River Romance

Stephanie's raft rounded a bend in the river and entered a red-walled canyon. There were a few rafts ahead of them, and a few behind.

"Stephanie, check out that canyon wall. See the way it sort of curves at the top?" Tim asked. "And look at that fantastic rock formation on the top of it. It looks almost like a little tower!"

Stephanie leaned forward to see what he was talking about. She spotted the curved wall, and then the rocks on top. "It seems ancient!" she commented. "Like an altar of some kind. Or maybe a lookout post, so they could see who was coming down the river."

Tim turned to her. "I bet you're right. Maybe we could do some exploring together—you know, separate from the trip."

Her heart lurched. "That would be . . . great," she said as she smiled at Tim. She could see them now: looking for arrowheads and artifacts in the moonlight, holding hands as they hopped over a small stream, gazing at constellations together, kissing . . .

She closed her eyes, picturing the perfect romantic moment.

"Stephanie!" someone screeched. *"Watch out!"*

FULL HOUSE™: Stephanie novels

Available from MINSTREL Books

FULL HOUSE™

Club Stephanie

Five Flamingo Summer

**Based on the hit Warner Bros.
TV series**

Kathy Clark

A Parachute Book

A MINSTREL® BOOK

Published by POCKET BOOKS
New York   London   Toronto   Sydney   Tokyo   Singapore

A MINSTREL PAPERBACK *Original*

 A Minstrel Book published by
POCKET BOOKS, a division of Simon & Schuster Inc.
1230 Avenue of the Americas, New York, NY 10020

A PARACHUTE BOOK

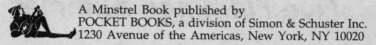 Copyright © and ™ 1999 by Warner Bros.

ISBN: 0-671-02157-5

First Minstrel Books printing May 1999

10 9 8 7 6 5 4 3 2 1

A MINSTREL BOOK and colophon are registered trademarks of Simon & Schuster Inc.

Cover photo by Schultz Photography

Printed in the U.S.A.

Five Flamingo Summer

CHAPTER

1

◆ ◣ ◢ ◆

"Wait a second, Steph—you're going to spend the summer trying to *survive?* And this is fun?" Uncle Jesse asked.

"The Super Summer Adventure isn't *all* about survival," Stephanie Tanner began to explain to her uncle.

Most of Stephanie's family was piled into the Tanner minivan. In just a few minutes they'd be dropping Stephanie off for a monthlong summer trip.

Stephanie twirled a strand of her long blond hair around a finger. "The point is to have all these different challenges and adventures, one after the other—and see if you can make it," she said.

"One adventure after another? I'm jealous!" Joey Gladstone cried. Joey, an old friend of Stephanie's father, lived in the Tanner household, too. "I wish I could go on a trip like that. I'd be great!"

D.J. Tanner, Stephanie's nineteen-year-old sister, laughed. "Joey, I read about some of the stuff Stephanie's doing over the summer. I bet you couldn't hack it," she teased. "River rafting, mountain climbing, wind surfing—"

"Oh, no. I forgot about the wind surfing." Stephanie's father, Danny Tanner, chewed his thumbnail nervously. "Steph, you're only fourteen—"

"Dad, I'll be *fine*," Stephanie said.

"Stephanie's ready for anything," D.J. said. "She inline skates all over the city—and that's when she's not riding her bike. She could practically pedal all the way from San Francisco to Los Angeles. Plus, lately she's become an even better swimmer than me." D.J. poked Stephanie in the arm.

"Thanks, Deej." Stephanie grinned at her older sister. She was going to miss her family over the summer. Stephanie had never been gone from home for so long. It was the middle of June, and she wouldn't get back to San Francisco until the third week of July.

Stephanie's mom had died when she was little.

Uncle Jesse and Joey had moved into the Tanner house to help Danny raise his three daughters. Then Jesse married Becky Donaldson, Danny's co-host on the morning TV show, *Wake Up, San Francisco*. When Becky and Jesse had twin boys, Alex and Nicky, Stephanie's full house, including Comet, the dog, was complete.

Everyone in Stephanie's family had come to see her off except Becky and the twins. They were visiting her parents for the week.

"Are you going to write us every day?" Stephanie's nine-year-old sister Michelle asked.

"Not quite," Stephanie said. "But I *am* going to write every day—in my journal. I saw this photo-journal in *Cool Adventure* magazine of a trip a girl took last summer. They publish one reader's journal every year. If mine is good enough, maybe they'll choose it! You brought your camera for me to borrow—right, Dad?"

Danny nodded. He motioned for Joey to open the glove compartment and pull out the camera. "Now, before I give this to you, remember what I said about keeping the lens clean with that special cloth."

"No problem," Stephanie said. Her father was an incredible neat freak. The day before, he had spent over two hours lecturing her on how to clean the camera—and only fifteen minutes on telling her how to get the best pictures. "I wrote down everything you told me."

"So can I *really* read your journal when you get back?" Michelle asked eagerly.

"Yes, Michelle—I told you already," Stephanie said. "You can read my journal."

Michelle pumped her fist in the air. "Yes! Finally!"

"It took you only five years of begging," D.J. commented under her breath.

"Sure, but five years that finally paid off!" Michelle answered.

Stephanie laughed. Michelle was always trying to get a look at her diaries. She sat up in her seat as the van pulled into the John Muir Middle School parking lot.

"There's Allie!" Michelle cried. She pointed to Stephanie's best friend since kindergarten, Allie Taylor. Allie had green eyes and wavy brown hair. She tended to be on the quiet side, and was very shy around boys.

Allie was standing with Darcy Powell, Anna Rice, and Kayla Norris—all of Stephanie's closest friends. Stephanie couldn't believe how lucky they were to be on the same trip. The sign-up process was first-come, first-serve—and there was even a waiting list!

Good thing I made everyone stay up late to write

out their applications at my sleepover back in March,
Stephanie thought. *Otherwise we would never all
have gotten in!* This trip was definitely a once-in-
a-lifetime opportunity.

As soon as Danny stopped the van, Stephanie
threw open the door. "Hey, guys—I'm here!" She
hopped out of the minivan and ran straight to
her friends.

"We were starting to wonder if you were coming," Darcy said. She was wearing long soccer
shorts and a T-shirt from her softball team's victory in the regional championships. It was pale
yellow and complemented Darcy's brown skin
perfectly. Darcy was an incredible athlete—she
was going to be great at the Super Summer
Adventure.

"We thought maybe you chickened out,"
Darcy kidded.

"What?" Stephanie punched Darcy's arm play-
fully. "No way, Darce. I am totally psyched
about this!"

"Me, too. Totally." Darcy grinned at Stephanie.

"You've been talking about this trip so much,
I'm surprised you didn't *sleep* in the parking lot,"
Anna teased. She adjusted the clasp of her beaded
necklace. She was wearing a sleeveless hand-
painted T-shirt, cut-off shorts, and leather sandals.
Anna made most of her own clothes, and Steph-

anie knew she'd become a fashion designer someday.

"I was going to, but my dad said no," Stephanie joked.

"I had the weirdest feeling when my mom and dad dropped me off," Allie said. "Like I was going into the army or something. I mean, all these outdoor adventures are going to be really hard." She curled her hair around her ear.

Allie hadn't been that excited about going on the trip at first. But when everyone else decided to go, Allie agreed to apply, too. How else would they get to spend the summer together?

Kayla put a hand on Allie's shoulder. "Don't worry. I bet you'll surprise yourself by how much you can do." Kayla was almost as good an athlete as Darcy—but she could be a klutz sometimes, too. She was tall and slim with long, blond hair.

"Stephanie! Way to totally ditch us in the parking lot!" Michelle called. She ran over, followed by the rest of Stephanie's family.

Stephanie stared. Joey and Jesse were actually holding a giant plastic banner that said WE'LL MISS YOU, STEPHAN. The banner ended there, the last two letters of her name cut off.

"Sorry. I made the letters a little too big," Michelle apologized. "Your whole name wouldn't fit."

"You should see the other side," D.J. joked. "She made it only as far as WE'LL MISS."

"Thanks, Michelle. I love it. Even if it *is* for someone named Stephan." Stephanie reached out to give Michelle a hug.

"Have fun, Steph!" D.J. squeezed Stephanie from the other side. "Meet lots of cute boys," she whispered.

Everyone in her family crowded around, giving her a group hug.

"I'll miss you guys," Stephanie said. Tears welled in her eyes. Even though she was totally excited about the trip, saying good-bye to her family was hard.

"We'll miss you more," Danny said softly. "So write every day." He paused. "Well, maybe that's too much. How about every other day?"

Stephanie wrinkled her nose. "How about once a week?"

Danny smiled. "And call us if you need anything. Hey, call us even if you don't. And especially call us as soon as you change your mind and decide not to do this crazy thing."

"*Dad.*" Stephanie rolled her eyes.

"Come on—my soccer game starts in five minutes!" Michelle yelled, running for the minivan.

Stephanie hugged her father again, then stood and watched as her whole huge family piled back into the van. Uncle Jesse pulled the van out of the parking lot and drove away.

"Wow! That was a lot harder than I thought it would be," she said after they left.

"I know," Kayla agreed. "I couldn't wait for my parents to leave me here, but when they did, I almost started bawling."

"Uh-oh." Darcy stood on her tiptoes. She looked across the parking lot. "I think I see another reason to start crying."

"What?" Stephanie followed her gaze.

"See that big maroon Jeep over there?" Darcy pointed. "Look who's getting *out* of it."

Stephanie nearly keeled over when she saw Darah Judson step out of the front passenger side of the Jeep. Darah was one of the leaders of a club called the Flamingoes. And the Flamingoes were bad news to Stephanie and her friends!

Back in the sixth grade, Stephanie had been asked to join the snobby, exclusive group. She turned them down, and they never forgave her. Since then the Flamingoes had tried everything possible to make Stephanie's life miserable. They'd spent the past two summers competing with Stephanie and her friends for jobs, for boys—and pretty much for everything. Stephanie couldn't think of anyone she'd rather see *less* than the Flamingoes just then!

"Maybe it's only Darah," Anna said. "Maybe she decided to try something new this summer and go on a trip by herself—"

"Then again, maybe *not*," Darcy said.

Stephanie followed her gaze. Tiffany Schroeder and Cynthia Hanson climbed out of the backseat of the Jeep. "Not Tiffany and Cynthia, too," she groaned.

"I can't imagine them on an adventure that didn't involve *shopping*," Allie quipped.

"Are they seriously planning to go on this trip?" Anna asked. "They'll be so lost! Well, Tiffany definitely!"

Stephanie couldn't believe it when Mikki Dior and Jenny Lyons climbed out of the car next. They were new members of the Flamingoes. Stephanie didn't know them well, but she *did* know they were as obnoxious as the rest.

Darcy giggled. "It looks like a clown's car in the circus. I mean, how many Flamingoes can *fit* into one car?"

"Shouldn't it be a pink car, anyway?" Anna said, wrinkling her nose. Pink was the Flamingoes' favorite color.

"Really." Darcy grimaced.

"Of all the summer programs around, why did the Flamingoes have to end up in *this* one?" Anna complained.

"Oh, great. They're coming this way," Allie said.

Stephanie took a deep breath. Whatever the Flamingoes were going to say to her, she didn't want to hear it. She knew that Darah had probably been saving up her best insults just to throw in Stephanie's face right now.

"Don't let them get to you," Darcy said through clenched teeth.

"I won't," Stephanie promised.

"Stephanie!" Darah cried as she moved closer.

Stephanie looked at her. "Yes, Darah?" she asked flatly.

Darah smiled. "How *are* you? I really missed you."

She threw her arms around Stephanie and gave her a big hug!

CHAPTER
2

◆ ◂ ◢ ◆

Stephanie stepped back, wriggling her way out of Darah's hug. *Whoa*, she thought. *Why is Darah acting like we're best friends?*

"It's so nice to see you guys," Darah said. She adjusted the pink headband in her long, dark brown hair. Mikki, Jenny, Tiffany, and Cynthia stood behind her.

"It is?" Stephanie raised her eyebrows.

"Oh, yeah. We were so afraid we wouldn't know anyone on the trip. And when we pulled up and saw you guys standing here, it was *such* a relief."

"It was?" Stephanie asked. She felt like reaching over and waving her hand in front of Darah's eyes. Did Darah realize whom she was talking to?

"Sure. We're going to have so much fun," Cynthia chimed in. She slid her pink-framed sunglasses down on her nose and peered over them. "I know *you'll* be ready for anything—right, Stephanie?" She clapped a hand on Stephanie's back.

Sure, I'm ready for anything. Anything but Flamingoes acting nice, Stephanie thought.

"Hey—I just had a brilliant idea," Tiffany said.

"I'll bet," Darcy said.

Stephanie bit her lip to keep from laughing.

"I think we should take before-and-after pictures—don't you, Cynthia? I want a photo of all of us on the day we left." Tiffany put her hands on Stephanie's shoulders and whirled her around.

"Wait a minute—" Stephanie heard the whir of a camera snapping a picture. "Why would you want a picture of my back?"

"Oh, man! I can't believe you guys!" Darcy looked at Stephanie's back.

"Can't believe what?" Stephanie asked.

"This!" Allie pulled a piece of paper off Stephanie's T-shirt.

Stephanie stared at the handwritten sign. YOU TOO CAN BE A NERD—ASK ME HOW! was printed in bold pink letters. She heard laughter and glanced at a group of boys standing nearby. They were all pointing at her.

12

Stephanie felt her face turn as pink as the Magic Marker the Flamingoes had used.

"Glad to see you've grown up so much over the past year," Darcy said to Tiffany.

"Yeah—I didn't know this trip was open to kindergartners," Stephanie added. "I could have invited my five-year-old nephews. I mean, if they were willing to take *you* guys . . ."

"Very funny. Have you been working on those jokes all year?" Jenny asked.

Tiffany tossed her perfectly cut blond hair over her shoulders. "You should have spent the time trying to figure out ways to look half as good as we do."

"Because right now, you don't." Cynthia glanced at Anna. "Are those clothes homemade? Or just cheap?"

Anna took a step toward Cynthia, as if she wanted to shove her. But Kayla grabbed her arm, holding her back. "Don't. If someone sees you, you could get kicked off the trip. And the Flamingoes aren't worth it," Kayla said.

The group of boys who'd been laughing at Stephanie's sign approached them. A tall boy with sandy hair and freckles smiled at Darah. "Nice sign! I'm glad there are some people on this trip who know how to have fun."

Darah gave him a cold look. "And you're fun?"

"Actually, I'm Bruce," he said, still smiling.

"And I'm thrilled," Darah told him. She turned to her friends. "Not!"

Bruce looked a little put off, but he didn't say anything. He turned to Stephanie. "Excuse me, but how exactly *do* I become a nerd?"

"Oh, I think you've got that covered already," Cynthia told him with a superior smile. Mikki and Jenny cracked up laughing.

Bruce's face turned red with anger.

"Forget her, dude," one of his friends said.

"No—don't bother. We'll forget *you*," Darah said. She beckoned to the other Flamingoes. "Let's go meet some of the *cool* people on this trip."

"Definitely," Mikki said, "because they're sure not over here!" She laughed as they walked away.

Stephanie looked at Bruce. Did he already dislike the Flamingoes as much as she did?

"Hey, Kevin—did you know there were going to be so many snobs on this trip?" Bruce asked one of his friends.

"They're unreal," Kevin said.

"Unfortunately, they're very real." Stephanie crumpled the handmade sign in her hand. "Real jerks!"

"Come on, guys. Let's go tell the counselors those girls need a van of their own," Bruce said.

14

"And maybe they can make it head in another direction!"

His friends laughed as they walked over to the counselors.

"This is a nightmare," Allie moaned.

"Yeah, and we can't even wake up," Kayla said. "It's one of those *living* nightmares. What are we going to do?"

Stephanie watched the Flamingoes work their way around the parking lot. She wouldn't be surprised if they were being rude and mean to everyone.

Well, there was no way she was letting the Flamingoes ruin everyone's summer adventure!

Stephanie watched Darah and Cynthia toss their luggage into the gear van. They brought twice as much as the trip leaders had suggested. They had so many clothes, it was ridiculous.

Stephanie grinned. She had a way to make the Flamingoes *really* miserable.

"Hey, guys, I have an idea," Stephanie said. "The Flamingoes won't go anywhere without a change of clothes or their makeup cases or their hair stuff, right?"

"They don't even go to *school* without that stuff," Darcy said. "But how can we—"

"I'm going to grab their bags from the gear van and leave them here," Stephanie announced.

15

"I don't know," Allie said. "Even the Flamingoes don't deserve to lose all their luggage."

"Someone will probably have their bags sent on," Stephanie explained. "But in the meantime, they'll feel totally grungy. That *might* make them hate outdoor adventuring enough to leave the trip behind. At least we'll enjoy watching them suffer for a few days."

"Watching the Flamingoes suffer?" Kayla grinned. "That *does* sound like fun."

"So how exactly are you going to pull this off, Stephanie?" Anna asked. "Won't somebody see you?"

"No—I'll just wait for the right time." Stephanie kept her eye on the van. The Flamingoes were busy talking to another group of boys.

A few minutes later the counselor who was packing the luggage van crossed to the other side of the parking lot. He began helping another counselor tie sleeping bags and tents on to a roof rack. Both their backs were turned.

"Here's my chance!" Stephanie said. "Wish me luck."

"Good luck," Darcy said, "and move fast!"

Stephanie skirted the edge of the lot. Within seconds she was standing at the rear of the gear van. Its back doors were wide open.

Stephanie took off her sunglasses and peered

inside. Her eyes quickly spotted a clump of pink. She grabbed the first three pink bags she saw and checked the ID tags.

DARAH JUDSON—GIRL EXTRAORDINAIRE was written on one tag. TIFFANY SCHROEDER—PRETTY AND PINK! was printed on another.

Stephanie tried not to gag as she hustled to stow the bags behind a large green bush. Trust the Flamingoes to have luggage tags with attitude!

She rushed back to the van and grabbed Mikki's and Jenny's bags. They were even heavier than the others, and she had to struggle to lift them from the van. Finally she dragged them over to the bush.

She turned around for the third and last load—Cynthia's stuff. Her heart gave a loud thump.

Standing between her and the van was a tall, angry-looking woman. A woman whose name tag said COUNSELOR in big black letters.

The woman glared at Stephanie. "What do you think *you're* doing?"

CHAPTER
3

◆ ◀ ◆ ◆

"Um, hi," Stephanie squeaked.

The woman folded her arms across her white T-shirt. Her long brown hair hung over one shoulder in a tight ponytail. "I asked what you were doing," she demanded.

"Loading luggage?" Stephanie suggested. She gave a weak smile.

The woman raised one eyebrow. "Looks more like *un*loading to me," she said.

Stephanie thought she seemed a little older than D.J. She was probably about twenty or twenty-one years old. Stephanie peered up at her name tag. GAIL PRESCOTT was printed in bold blue Magic Marker. Right above the word *counselor*.

"Well? What do you have to say for yourself?"

Gail demanded. "And where's your name tag? You're supposed to be wearing it."

Stephanie pulled the plastic tag out of her pocket and held it up for Gail to read. Then she pinned it to her green polo shirt.

"Stephanie Tanner. Hmm. I'll make a note of that," Gail said. She jotted something down on her clipboard. "I'm letting this slide—after you get the bags back in the van. But I'm warning you, if anything strange happens to anyone's luggage, I'll know whom to talk to about it."

"But I was only—see, I—" Stephanie fumbled for words. How could she explain the rivalry between her friends and the Flamingoes?

"You were only *ditching* our luggage!"

Stephanie turned. Darah walked up, followed by the rest of the Flamingoes. "We saw you pulling our bags off the van, so don't try to deny it!"

"How could you do that to us? We've never done anything to *you*," Tiffany said in a soft, innocent-sounding voice.

"What?" Stephanie couldn't believe her ears. "You've got to be kidding!"

"How about that sign you just plastered on Stephanie's back?" Allie asked. Darcy, Kayla, and Anna walked up right behind her.

"Wait! Hold on a second. Could somebody tell me what's going on?" Gail asked, arms still folded in front of her. "You just got here, so how come you're already arguing?"

"I can explain everything," Stephanie said. At least, she hoped so. "See, Darah and her friends and me and my friends—well, we don't get along that well. Which I personally was willing to totally forget. I mean, put aside our differences and all. Except as soon as they got here, they started making fun of me. I had been here only five minutes, when they put a stupid sign on my back. Calling me a nerd."

"What sign?" Jenny gazed around at her friends with a confused expression.

Stephanie seethed. "The sign that was just on my back!"

"Oh, please," Darah said. "As if we'd do something so dumb!"

"You would, and you did," Anna said. "How can you stand here and deny it?"

"Because it's simply not true," Darah said. "And, Stephanie, I'm surprised you'd make up a story when we haven't seen each other in a long time, and we were just getting reacquainted—"

"Yeah, reacquainted with how incredibly mean you guys can be," Darcy said.

"Do you hear this?" Cynthia asked the counselor. She put her hands on her hips as if she were outraged. "Can you believe the name calling, and the rudeness, and—"

"You're the ones who labeled Stephanie with a nerd sign!" Allie said.

Gail formed a T with her hands. "Whoa, girls—timeout! That's enough for now. More than enough, actually," she added. "I can tell you don't get along that well, and that's something we'll need to work on. But in the meantime, I can act only on what I see. And, Stephanie, it seems as though you're the only troublemaker here. You were caught red-handed."

Gail frowned at Stephanie. "I think you'd better take this trip a little more seriously. Unless, of course, you'd rather not go at all. And if you pull any more stunts, going home *is* an option. Remember that."

Stephanie gulped. Gail was threatening to send her home—and the trip hadn't even started yet.

"Nothing like this will happen again—I promise," Stephanie assured her.

"Could I have your attention? Attention, everyone!" Another counselor, a petite woman with curly blond hair, blew a whistle. "Could you all please come over here so we can assign you to the right van?"

"Assigned to vans? Don't we get to sit where we want?" Tiffany complained.

"We want you all to make new friends this summer," Gail told her as they walked over to join the larger group.

Stephanie looked around her at the other campers. She knew there were forty in all—twenty boys and twenty girls—and eight counselors. She wouldn't mind making some new friends. She'd be glad to hang out with anyone *but* the Flamingoes!

"My name's Molly, and I'd like to welcome you to Super Summer Adventure," the petite blond woman said. She smiled at the crowd. "I hope you're all ready for the most exciting time of your life! We have some great challenges for you this summer—hiking, mountain biking, wind surfing—"

She was interrupted by cheers and whistles from the campers.

"And our first Super Summer Adventure Super Challenge, white-water rafting!" Molly continued. "But first we have a long bus trip ahead of us. So listen up while I tell you where to go."

Molly ran through the lists of the campers and counselors. When she was finished, she told them who would ride in which van. There were four vans for campers and counselors, plus one van for gear.

The one person Stephanie did know in her assigned van was Tiffany. And she didn't plan on sitting anywhere near her!

"See you at the first rest stop!" Stephanie called to her friends as she walked off to her van. She had to wait for a few kids ahead of her to board the van.

She climbed up after them and stood in the doorway for a few seconds. When her eyes adjusted to the light, she saw a cute boy with short, blond hair sitting in the back row.

"Hurry up. We need to get going," one of the counselors urged Stephanie from behind.

"Okay, I'm hurrying," Stephanie said. *At least, I am now!* She smiled and started walking back.

She passed Tiffany and then Bruce. Stephanie kept going to the back row. She gazed down at the blond-haired boy, who was busy reading a book. The title on the cover was *Happiness and the Art of Success*.

Wow, Stephanie thought, *what a serious book.*

Suddenly the boy looked up. She felt her heart lurch. He had the brightest blue eyes she had ever seen. He gazed at her so intently, she felt as though he were hypnotizing her.

Stephanie swallowed hard. Her palms began to sweat. *He is totally gorgeous!* she thought.

"Hi, I'm Stephanie," she said. She could barely get the words out. "Stephanie Tanner."

"Hey. My name's Tim Bennett." He gestured to the seat beside him. "Want to sit down?"

"Thanks." Stephanie sat down next to Tim.

Forget about the Flamingoes ruining things, she thought. *This summer is getting off to a great start— as of now!*

CHAPTER
4

◆ ◂ ◆ ◆

Tim turned to Stephanie after the van cruised on to the highway, headed east. "I saw you outside before." He grinned.

"You did?" Stephanie felt herself blush. He'd already noticed her? Maybe that meant he thought she was cute, too.

"Yeah, I saw you taking those girls' bags," Tim said.

Stephanie gulped. That wasn't exactly something she wanted to be known for!

"You were putting their luggage behind a bush when my dad dropped me off," Tim explained. "I couldn't figure out what you were doing."

"Oh!" Stephanie laughed nervously. *"That."* She gave a little wave of her hand. "That was nothing."

"I mean, did you need more room in the van for your own stuff," Tim went on, "or were you playing a practical joke?"

Stephanie chewed her lower lip. How was she going to explain this? She realized now that she might have gone overboard when she hijacked the Flamingoes' luggage.

"Actually, see, those girls and I, we kind of go back a long way. They always harass me and my friends. For the past few summers, we've been having this feud. They do stuff to us—practical jokes, pranks—and then we have to get them back, retaliate . . ."

"I don't get it." Tim shook his head. "I mean, why can't you just be friends?"

Stephanie lowered her sunglasses and looked Tim in the eye. "You don't *know* them." She glanced at Tiffany in the front row of the van. "They're the most self-centered, rudest—"

Bruce glanced over his shoulder at Stephanie.

She smiled at him, then continued speaking to Tim in a softer voice. "Anyway, they're bad news."

"Okay, okay, I get the picture," Tim said. "But isn't it sort of pointless to spend your time worrying about what *they're* going to do next? And then reacting to it?"

"Well . . . I guess," Stephanie said slowly. Now

that he put it that way, it did sound like a dumb way to spend the summer. Especially when she'd be traveling all over the West. And when she could be spending time with Tim instead.

"Arguing and fighting can be a real waste of time," Tim observed. "Sometimes it's better just to walk away."

"Walk away?" Stephanie looked at Tim. "But wouldn't that mean losing? Giving in?"

Tim shrugged. "Maybe if you quit reacting to them, they'd quit, too," he said. "Then you could concentrate on having *fun* instead. That's why we're here, right? That's why I'm here, anyway."

"You're totally right. But do you really think they'd stop?" Stephanie asked.

Tim nodded. "It's all in this book I'm reading. There's a section on how not to let your opponent get to you. The secret is to ignore the other guy and focus on yourself. Eventually you'll come out on top. I was hoping this book would help me in sports."

Stephanie thought about it. "But in sports you can't ignore what your opponent is doing."

"Not in all sports," Tim agreed. "But think of it as a free throw in basketball. You know how you're at the line. And all the fans in the bleachers are waving their hands to distract you so you'll miss?"

27

Stephanie nodded. She'd watched enough games to know what he meant.

"But you have to concentrate and think of all the thousands of times you've sunk free throws," Tim went on. "And you can't let the fans affect you. Well, that's how I think when someone gets in my way or provokes me. I just keep my cool."

Stephanie liked what Tim was saying, but she couldn't help feeling a little skeptical. "What if someone's mean to you? Would you really let them get away with it?"

"Sure." Tim shrugged. "Why not? What have I got to lose?"

"People might call you chicken," Stephanie said.

"So? I know that I'm not," Tim said. His eyes gleamed with excitement. "I'm just saving my energy for things I *want* to do. Like all the adventures on this trip!"

Stephanie gazed thoughtfully at Tim. Maybe it was possible to be strong and stand up for yourself without fighting back. But could Stephanie really act that way around the Flamingoes?

"Tim—could I borrow that book?" she asked. "I think I'd like to find out more about that stuff."

"You can read it now." Tim handed her the book.

"Thanks." Stephanie glanced at the back cover.

"Wow, the guy who wrote this was on the United States Olympic gold medal hockey team!"

Tim nodded.

"Do you play hockey?" Stephanie asked.

"Usually right after basketball practice," Tim admitted with a sheepish grin. "I'm kind of a sports nut."

"Wow! I like sports, too," Stephanie said eagerly. "It's amazing."

"What is?" Tim asked.

"Oh—just . . ." Stephanie wished she hadn't said anything. What was she going to say next? That they had the same interests? That even though she had just met Tim, she felt as if she'd known him a long time? She was going to sound so dumb!

Better say something else, she decided.

"This *trip* is amazing. Getting to try all these new sports. I'm really looking forward to all the challenges." *And to spending more time with you*, she added silently.

"Yeah. I can't wait to go white-water rafting," Tim said. "Rapids, here we come!" His eyes brightened. "You *are* going to raft with me, aren't you?"

Her heart flipped over. "Of course!" Stephanie grinned as she scrunched down in her seat to get comfortable. She was so happy she had met Tim!

Instead of worrying about the Flamingoes, she couldn't wait for the first adventure of the summer.

This is exactly how I pictured it, Stephanie thought. *Cruising down the highway, sitting next to a cute boy . . . only Tim's even cuter than the boy I imagined!*

The vans pulled into a campground at seven o'clock that night. The groups split into girls and boys to set up camp for the night. Stephanie said good-bye to Tim, then rushed to find her friends.

"You guys! Hey, how are you?" Stephanie dropped her backpack next to theirs. They'd chosen an area underneath a tall fir tree to pitch their tents.

"Isn't the fresh air here incredible?" Anna took a deep breath. "It's like we're miles and miles from the city already."

Darcy laughed. "That's because we are!"

Stephanie stretched her arms over her head and gazed through the trees at the sky above her. "I love being out here."

"So, did you meet anyone on your van, Steph?" Kayla asked.

"You won't believe it, but I met the *cutest* guy. His name's Tim—"

"And you're in love already," Allie said with a laugh. "I can hear it in your voice!"

"I'm not in love. I just like him, that's all," Stephanie said. She described Tim and his book.

"And so after thinking about it, I realized—that's exactly what we need to do," Stephanie cried. "We need to forget about the Flamingoes."

"Well, sure—if they weren't on this *trip*, we could!" Darcy said.

"Even *with* them here," Stephanie argued. "We need to rise above our silly squabbles with them. If they pick fights with us, we ignore them. If they try to be better than us, we don't care. In short, we simply don't think about the Flamingoes. Our own lives are more important. So, what do you say? Are you with me? Let's make this the summer we forget about fighting with Flamingoes!" Stephanie threw her fist into the air.

Four stunned faces stared back at her.

"Are you serious?" Allie made a face.

Anna turned to Kayla. "Was that Stephanie Tanner talking?"

"I think sitting in a van all day must have scrambled her brain," Darcy said. "Either that or she's fallen in love and can't see straight. Are you feeling all right, Steph?"

"Yes! I feel fine," Stephanie said with a laugh. "Better than ever, in fact. Because once and for all, I know the solution to our problems with the Flamingoes."

"So you keep saying." Anna sounded doubtful.

"Yes. If we ignore them, they'll go away," Stephanie said confidently. "Tim told me that whenever they start to bother me, I can think serene thoughts until the irritation passes."

"But the irritations aren't going anywhere," Darcy commented. "In fact, it looks like they're planning on sleeping right over there." She pointed to where the Flamingoes were sitting in a circle, on their backpacks.

"Forget about them," Stephanie pleaded. "Pretend they're not there."

"Stephanie . . . I don't know if I can buy this from you," Anna said. "Are you telling me that if a Flamingo came up behind you right now and pasted a nerd sign on your back, you'd just smile and wait for her to go away?"

"Exactly!" Stephanie stated. "I'm so glad you understand."

"I don't understand anything," Darcy said. "A few hours ago you were plotting Stephanie's last revenge. And now you're going to trade revenge for *serene thoughts?*"

"Look. It's going to be an incredible trip, with all these adventures. Why do we even want to bother with the Flamingoes?" Stephanie argued.

"I guess you have a point," Allie agreed.

"Another bonus—if we don't fight with the Flamingoes, Gail will be happy. She'll forget we ever caused any trouble. Which will make the trip a lot more fun, right?" Stephanie asked.

"True . . ." Kayla said.

Darcy put her hands on her hips. "I'll make you a bet, Stephanie," she said. "I'll bet you, you can't be nice to the Flamingoes for one whole week. If I lose, I'll pack up your tent and backpack every morning for the rest of the trip. If you lose, you'll do the same for me."

"You're on!" Stephanie exclaimed. "But on one condition. You have to get along with them, too."

"I'll *try* it your way," Darcy said. "But that's all I can promise right now. I want to see how long *you* can make it, Steph."

"I'll make it," Stephanie declared. "Don't worry about me!"

Stephanie couldn't wait to tell Tim that thanks to him, the long war was over. *From this day on,* she vowed silently, *I have a new policy: Mind over Flamingoes!*

CHAPTER
5

♦ ◀ ◆ ♦

"Hey, you guys?" Molly stopped in front of Stephanie and her friends.

Stephanie and the other campers had just finished eating homemade stew around the campfire. They were camping by a small pond that was fed by a gurgling stream. Stephanie had spent dinner getting to know some of the other girls on the trip. She was having a great time so far.

"What's up?" Stephanie asked Molly.

"Well, I know you're all friends and probably want to hang out together tonight. But the tents are for two people. That means you have an extra person. And Cynthia needs a tentmate, too. So I was wondering who will share with her?" Molly smiled at Kayla.

"Um, no one?" Allie mumbled to Stephanie.

Stephanie nodded in agreement. Share a tent with Cynthia? Even sleeping outside on the ground with no protection would be better.

"Well, count me out," Kayla said under her breath. "Calling a truce is one thing. Living in the same tent is another."

"No kidding," Anna said. "I bet Cynthia wouldn't even make room for someone else's sleeping bag."

Stephanie was about to ask Molly if there were any extra tents, when she spotted Tim across the clearing. He was adjusting a stake on his tent.

Hadn't she just decided to follow Tim's advice and forget about the Flamingoes? Or at least try to get along with them for the summer. Sharing a tent with Cynthia was the perfect way to show Tim—and her friends—she was serious about ending this dumb feud.

"Molly—" Stephanie began.

"I'll share with Cynthia," Darcy cut in. "It's no problem." She picked up her sleeping bag and foam ground pad.

"What?" Stephanie asked. "But I was about to say—"

"It's okay," Darcy told her. "I'll do it. If we're going to call off the war, I might as well make the first move. Maybe Cynthia and I will find out we actually have something in common."

"Don't count on it," Anna said. "Unless you've become vain and self-centered in the last half hour."

"Cynthia can't be that bad all the time," Darcy said. "Maybe she's different when she's not around Darah."

"All right, Darcy." Stephanie smiled. She was glad that someone else was taking a positive approach to their summer with the Flamingoes. "Way to go!"

Stephanie watched as Darcy walked over to where Cynthia was crouched beside the tent, staring at all the stakes scattered around her feet. The nylon tent fabric was bunched up in a ball beside her. "Hey, Cynthia—want some help putting up your tent?" Darcy offered. "We'd better hurry, it'll be dark soon."

"Don't do me any favors," Cynthia said.

"It's the least I can do, considering I'll be sleeping here, too." Darcy lifted a corner of the tent.

"*You're* the one I have to share with?" Cynthia sputtered.

Darcy smiled at her. "I won't take up any more room than anyone else, I promise."

"Oh, great. Just great," Cynthia grumbled. "This is so exactly not what I need right now."

Darcy looked over at Stephanie and shrugged.

"Keep trying," Stephanie mouthed.

"I can't believe Darcy volunteered like that," Kayla said. She and Stephanie quickly pitched their tent. "She's setting herself up for disaster."

"Not necessarily. I bet it'll work out fine—as long as she keeps a positive attitude," Stephanie predicted.

She and Kayla unrolled their sleeping bags onto foam mats. Then they set their packs inside the tent and started getting out the things they needed for the night.

"I'm going to get ready for bed," Kayla said. "I guess I'll change clothes in my sleeping bag."

"I'm going to the water pump to brush my teeth." Stephanie held up her toothbrush. "Be back in two minutes."

"If you're not, I'll call the bear patrol," Kayla teased.

"More like the mosquito police." Stephanie swatted at one that had just landed on her arm. She stuck her toothbrush in her mouth and walked over to the water pump. The sky was almost completely dark. The first stars twinkled above the treetops. Stephanie was glad she had brought her flashlight.

She had just finished brushing her teeth and was turning to walk back to her tent, when she heard someone else using the pump. She spun around, bouncing the flashlight beam off the red pump handle.

"Tim?" she said. "Is that you?"

"Yef, it'f me—toofpafte in mouf," Tim mumbled.

Stephanie laughed. "Hey, how's it going? No—don't tell me now. Wait until you can actually talk."

Tim rinsed his mouth. "Hi, Stephanie. Kind of weird to be brushing your teeth in the great outdoors, huh?" he asked.

Stephanie laughed. "It reminds me of all my family's camping trips. For years I was convinced that mountain lions were waiting to attack me as soon as I stepped outside the tent. I never wanted to brush my teeth after dark."

"Did you ever *see* any lions?" Tim asked.

"No. But I saw a chipmunk once. You should have heard me scream." Stephanie laughed. "Actually, you probably *could* have—a thousand miles away!"

Tim laughed. "Chipmunks *can* be scary, can't they?"

Stephanie giggled. "Well, hopefully I'll be a little calmer on this trip."

"You will be," Tim agreed. "It's a plan." He smiled at Stephanie.

She felt her heart skip a beat. It was almost as if they were the only two people in the world.

"Excuse me," a voice behind her said. "Could you move and let someone *else* have some water?"

Stephanie stepped backward, shining her flashlight at the figure behind her. The figure was wearing pink pajamas. "Go ahead, Mikki," she said. "I'm sorry."

"Yeah. Sure you are," Mikki grumbled. She held her toothbrush under the pump and pulled the lever. Nothing happened. She pushed the button on the drinking fountain. No water came out. She turned to Stephanie. "Oh, great. Now you broke this thing?"

"Actually, you just need to pump up some more water," Stephanie told her. "Here, I'll do it."

"Is this a trick?" Mikki eyed Stephanie warily.

"No. We just used up the water." Stephanie lifted the large green handle and pushed it down. She repeated the movement several times. "Stand back, Mikki. It'll come out fast."

Mikki took a few steps back as Stephanie lifted the knob to release water. "There you go," she said cheerfully.

"Gee, thanks," Mikki said.

Stephanie shrugged. "We're going to miss

water when we start rafting. There won't be any drinkable water except what we carry with us."

"Hello, we'll *be* on a river." Mikki rubbed her hands under the tap.

"Didn't you read all the stuff they sent us? You can't drink river water," Tim told her. "It has bacteria in it."

"Oh." Mikki brushed her hair back. "Well, whatever." She finished cleaning up and then retreated to her tent.

"I guess not everyone's prepared for this summer," Tim mused once she was gone. "Me—I went out and read everything I could find about the areas we'll be visiting. This is a once-in-a-lifetime trip—"

"That's exactly how I feel," Stephanie cut in. "Sorry. It's just nice to know that someone else is as excited as I am." *And that's another thing we have in common*, Stephanie thought. *The list is getting longer and longer!*

"Definitely," Tim agreed. He smiled at her.

Oh, no—not that smile again, Stephanie thought. *I think I'll probably melt!* "Well, uh, good night. I'll see you tomorrow," she told him.

"In the van all day, but then the next day we'll be on the river—I can't wait," Tim said.

"Neither can I," Stephanie told him. "Good night!"

Stephanie smiled all the way back to her tent. Tim had kind of said he couldn't wait to see her again! She felt the same way. In fact, she was practically counting the minutes.

"What are you smiling about?" Kayla asked as Stephanie slipped back into the tent. She was sitting on her sleeping bag and reading with a flashlight.

Stephanie zipped the door closed. "I ran into Tim," she said in a soft voice. "He's so sweet! He actually said he couldn't wait to see me tomorrow. And we have so much in common. How much we like camping, and sports, and how we want this to be a perfect summer."

"Wow. You guys are really hitting it off." Kayla turned off the flashlight. She snuggled into her sleeping bag.

"Tim seems pretty different from the other boys I've liked," Stephanie mused.

"Different? How?" Kayla asked.

"Just the way he looks at things. He's serious, but he's also laid-back. He's intense about sports," Stephanie said as she got into her sleeping bag. "He's funny. He loves a challenge."

"Speaking of challenges—did you tell him you decided to leave the Flamingoes alone this summer?" Kayla asked.

"Sort of," Stephanie said.

"I bet when he finds out how much you've listened to his ideas—he'll be so flattered," Kayla said.

"I was really nice to Mikki just now. And Tim was standing right there," Stephanie said. "Not that *she* noticed. She was as rude as ever."

"Well, keep trying, I guess," Kayla said in a sleepy voice.

"I will," Stephanie promised. "Good night." She closed her eyes and pictured Tim's smile.

Stephanie drifted off to sleep thinking of Tim. She had just started dreaming about him, when a high-pitched scream startled her awake.

She sat up, knocking her head into the flashlight hanging from the tent ceiling. "Ouch!" she muttered. She grabbed the flashlight and turned it on.

"What was that?" Beside her, Kayla sat up and rubbed her eyes sleepily. "Did somebody scream?"

"I heard a shriek. I hope everyone's okay!" Stephanie pulled on a sweatshirt and unzipped the tent flap. Standing outside, she shone the flashlight around at all the tents.

Cynthia was standing in the clearing. She was holding her sleeping bag upside down and shaking it furiously.

"Cynthia? Did you scream?" Stephanie stared

42

at two green frogs in front of Cynthia on the ground. *How did those get there?* she wondered.

"What is it? Cynthia, what's wrong?" Gail ran up. She shone her flashlight at Cynthia's sleeping bag.

"Do you have ants in there or something?" Tiffany asked. Her flashlight cast a beam of pink light around the clearing. "I hate ants. I hate when you're having a picnic and—"

Ribbit. A green frog dropped from the bottom of the sleeping bag. *Ribbit!* it croaked, louder this time.

"Go *away!*" Cynthia hopped from one foot to the other. "See? I told you!"

Stephanie giggled. Everyone around her started laughing, too. The way Cynthia was jumping around, she looked just like a frog! Everyone was shining their flashlights at her.

There just might be enough light for a picture! Stephanie thought. She reached back into her tent and pulled out her camera. Then she turned on the flash and focused. She clicked three quick shots of Cynthia as more frogs fell out of her sleeping bag.

"Ick! That's disgusting!" Darah cried. "How could you possibly have so many frogs in there?"

"It's like a colony or something," Mikki said, her face almost as green as the frogs.

"What's going on here?" Gail demanded.

"What's going on is that Stephanie and her friends thought it would be cute to put fifty frogs in my sleeping bag," Cynthia said.

"We didn't think anything like that," Kayla protested.

"Anyway, it sure wasn't *fifty*," Darcy said. "Five, maybe."

"Well, you would know!" Cynthia screamed. "Now I know why you volunteered to share a tent with me. So you could sabotage me!"

"What? I did not!" Darcy said.

"What's happening?" Bruce walked into the clearing. "We heard you scream clear across the campground."

"Ever think about singing opera?" his friend Kevin asked. They snickered. "Really *bad* opera?"

"All right, everyone. Leave Cynthia alone, please," Gail said. "She's obviously been through enough tonight." She turned to Stephanie. "And I don't think she needs to get that close to nature again. Do you understand?"

"Do *I* understand?" Stephanie sputtered. "But I didn't have anything to do with this. At all! I'd never put frogs in someone's sleeping bag. That's so childish."

"Childish? This from the same person who

tried to take our bags and hide them behind some bushes?" Darah asked.

"I have no idea who's responsible here," Gail said. "But I do know that we won't put up with any more pranks." She stared directly at Stephanie. "You tried something earlier today, and I sincerely hoped you wouldn't try anything else."

"Gail—Cynthia—I promise," Stephanie said forcefully, "I had nothing to do with this. I'm through with silly pranks and games—ask any of my friends!"

"Like we trust *them?*" Darah scoffed.

"It's true," Kayla said. "Stephanie made a vow today not to bother you guys anymore. And besides that, we were both in our tent. She couldn't have stuffed frogs into your sleeping bag. She didn't have time."

"Not true!" Mikki said. "I saw her at the water pump, so she wasn't in your tent *all* night."

Stephanie winced. Why was this turning into a trial all of a sudden? She wasn't responsible! But how could she make everyone—especially Gail—believe her?

"Well, as much as I'd like to iron this all out, we have a big day ahead of us," Gail said. "I want everyone to go back to bed. Cynthia, let's get you a spare sleeping bag. We carry extras in case of emergency. Come with me. Everyone else, to bed right away." Gail and Cynthia headed across the clearing to one of the gear vans.

"What do you think that was all about?" Kayla asked. She and Stephanie headed back to their tent. "Poor Darcy. Cynthia will make her check the tent constantly for frogs now."

Stephanie grinned. Then her grin faded as she remembered how hard Darcy had laughed at the sight of all those frogs.

Was Cynthia right? Had Darcy volunteered to share a tent with Cynthia so she could scare her? Darcy hadn't seemed convinced by Stephanie's new mind over Flamingoes approach. And she did bet Stephanie that Stephanie couldn't keep the peace.

Stephanie shook her head. Surely Darcy wouldn't stir things up between Stephanie and the Flamingoes just so she could win her bet.

Would she?

CHAPTER
6

◆ ◀ ▪ ◆

The next morning Stephanie picked up her towel, her sack of toiletries, and Tim's book before heading over to the campsite showers. She knew there'd be a long line, so she planned to read while she waited. She didn't care how long it took, as long as there was hot water left. She had never felt so grubby in her life. Her baseball cap felt as if it were permanently attached to her head.

The path ran along a rocky cliff. Stephanie stopped to gaze at the tree-covered valley before her. The pine-scented air smelled so fresh! Yesterday they had driven all the way from San Francisco to the Humboldt National Forest in eastern Nevada. Today they would drive almost as far, to reach the Yampa River in Colorado. *Now, that will be real wilderness*, Stephanie thought excitedly.

As she passed by the tents on the other side of the campground, she heard someone say her name. She looked around. The voice was coming from inside a tent.

Stephanie closed her eyes. Now she recognized the voice. It was Tim's!

"I have no idea why girls do that," Stephanie heard Tim saying. "I guess they think it helps or something."

"Well, it doesn't," another boy said. Stephanie recognized the voice. It belonged to Dylan, Tim's tent mate. "It makes me nervous. I feel like they want something from me."

"Yeah, I know what you mean," Tim said. "When someone comes on too strong, it's like . . . whoa! Back off. Right?"

Dylan laughed. "Back *way* off, dude, is what I say."

Stephanie stopped in her tracks. Tim said he didn't like girls who came on too strong. Was he talking about her? She sat next to Tim in the van. She sat next to him at dinner the night before. She talked to him at the water pump. Did Tim think *she* was coming on too strong?

Stephanie hurried past his tent without saying hello. She took her place at the end of the line. There was no way she was going to talk to Tim now. Maybe from now on, she shouldn't talk to him unless *he* spoke first.

Stephanie moved forward a few steps with the line. She started leafing through Tim's book. There were a few sections she wanted to reread.

"Hey—still reading?"

Stephanie snapped the book closed and found herself face-to-face with Tim. "Um, yeah." She smiled nervously. Then she forced herself to stop smiling. That might be too much.

"Which section are you up to?" Tim asked.

"Chapter nine," Stephanie said.

Tim seemed to be waiting for her to say more. Finally he asked, "And what do you think?"

"It's good." Stephanie nodded.

There was another awkward pause. Stephanie wanted to thank Tim for lending her the book. She wanted to tell him that it really struck a chord with her. But she couldn't—that might seem like she was coming on too strong again.

"So, is the line moving at all?" Tim asked.

Stephanie shrugged. "Kind of." She chewed her thumbnail. *Not* talking to Tim was a lot harder than talking to him.

"Well, I guess all we can do is wait," Tim said. "I wish I'd brought a book, too."

"Do you want to look through this again?" Stephanie asked.

"Oh, no—that's okay. You're reading it," Tim said.

"What are you reading?"

Stephanie turned around. Cynthia was standing behind her. She peered at the cover of Stephanie's book. *"Happiness and the Art of Success?* That doesn't sound too fascinating."

"Actually, it is," Stephanie told her calmly. Now was the perfect time to show Tim how she wasn't going to let Cynthia bother her.

Tim stepped around Stephanie. "It's my book, actually. I'm really into self-improvement stuff."

"Oh, yeah? Me, too," Cynthia said.

"Really?" Tim asked. "Like what?"

"Like I spent hours last week experimenting with different hairstyles." Cynthia patted her long, blond hair. "And I just found a new exercise for my stomach muscles."

Tim smiled. "Well, I don't mean just looking better. The book is about being a better person all around—making the most of yourself."

"Now, that *does* sound interesting." Cynthia laughed. "Like being a better all-around athlete. You know what I should do? Borrow that book when Stephanie's done with it. Then maybe I'd have some clue. If you're into it, Tim, I'm sure it's cool."

Stephanie smiled politely. "You can read it as soon as I'm done," she promised Cynthia.

Stephanie opened her book and started reading. If Cynthia was going to stand there and flirt with Tim, Stephanie needed all the extra help on serenity she could get.

Stephanie focused on the page in front of her. *When you feel like striking back, don't. The true path to victory does not include negative detours. Walk in a straight line. You will reach your goal more quickly.*

Kayla strode out of the girls' shower. "Next!" she shouted. She waved to Stephanie.

"Enjoy," Tim said.

"Actually, I can wait." Stephanie shrugged. "Cynthia, do you want to go ahead of me?" she offered. "You've been dying for a hot shower." *And I'm dying not to listen to you any longer*, Stephanie added silently.

"Totally," Cynthia agreed. "So I can wash all the frog slime off me." She glared at Stephanie.

"I can imagine," Stephanie said brightly. "Go ahead. I'll go after you."

"Okay. Thanks, I guess." Cynthia picked up her tube of shampoo and shuffled toward the showers in her pink sandals.

Tim turned to face Stephanie. She smiled awkwardly.

"That was really nice of you," Tim said. "I hope Cynthia appreciates it."

"Oh. Um, thanks. I think she did," Stephanie said. "Anyway, what's five minutes? I don't mind waiting." *But I do mind pretending I don't want to talk to you—when that's all I want to do.*

Stephanie finally got to shower about ten minutes later. As she came out of the shower, Tim was nowhere in sight. But the rest of the Flamingoes were standing impatiently by the door.

Tiffany peered around the corner into the small, steamy shower area. "*This* is the shower Cynthia was talking about?"

"I'd rather bathe in the freezing cold river," Darah said. "At least that would be remotely clean."

"You guys have sandals on," Stephanie pointed out. "It's not like your feet will have to touch the cement floor."

"Cement? That's disgusting," Jenny said.

"I can't believe the conditions they expect us to live in," Mikki complained. "I mean, they're practically barbaric."

"Medieval," Jenny agreed.

"What were you guys expecting, the Hilton?" Bruce joked as he came out of the boys' shower.

"It's not that bad," Stephanie said. "Remember—we won't be getting regular showers for the next few days. It's now or never."

"I'll go first!" Tiffany pushed past the other Flamingoes.

Stephanie ran a comb through her wet hair and started to walk back toward her tent.

"Stephanie! Hey, you left your camera on a tree stump by your tent. I just found it." Darcy jogged up and held the camera out to Stephanie.

Stephanie grimaced. "Oh, no. I put it there after I took pictures of Cynthia and the frogs last night. If my dad knew I left it out—"

"Overnight, on a dirty tree stump, no less." Darcy shook her head. "You'd be grounded for a year!"

"Please make sure you never mention this to him," Stephanie said, prying off the lens cap. "Ever!" She held the camera and looked through the viewfinder. She focused on the Flamingoes in line for the shower. "You know, this would make a great photo—"

"Agh! Ick-ick-ick, noooooooooo!" A screech came out of the girls' shower room.

"What in the world . . . who's that?" Darcy stared at the showers.

Stephanie gazed through the camera's viewfinder at the shower entrance. Seconds later Tiffany came flying out. She was wrapped in a large beach towel. Her skin and hair had turned completely green! A glob of green gel sat on top of her head.

Everyone standing outside burst out laughing. The always perfectly put together Tiffany looked like a creature that had just crawled out of a swampy lagoon!

Stephanie couldn't resist. She snapped a photo. Tiffany glared at her. "This is all your fault, Stephanie!" she cried.

CHAPTER
7

◆ ◀ ◗ ◆

"*Me?* What did I do?" Stephanie asked.

"Tiffany? Stephanie? Is there a problem here?"

At the sound of Gail's voice, Stephanie felt the hairs prickle on the back of her neck. Not again! Out of the corner of her eye, she saw other campers running up to see what was going on.

"Yes, there's a problem. *Her!*" Tiffany pointed at Stephanie.

"I didn't do anything," Stephanie protested. "I have no idea what happened to you, Tiffany."

"Oh, really. You have no idea how *green* water came out of the shower and on to my head!" Tiffany yelled.

Stephanie shrugged. "No, I don't."

"Well, that's probably because you got your

friends to do it for you," Tiffany said. "You took a shower right before me, so you must have rigged it with green goo."

"Tiffany, don't be ridiculous. I wouldn't know *how* to do something like that," Stephanie argued. "Even if I wanted to—"

"Ah-ha! So you wanted to," Tiffany said. "Admit it!"

"No, honestly!" Stephanie cried. "Why would you think that?"

"Gee, I don't know. Because you've done dumb stunts like this in the past—like, the very recent past?" Darah suggested. "Don't you remember putting frogs in Cynthia's sleeping bag last night? And stealing our luggage?"

"Taking your bags was a big mistake, I admit it," Stephanie said. "But I made a vow not to do anything like that ever again."

"Well, you obviously broke your so-called vow. But don't worry. You can forget about tricking us in the future," Tiffany said. "Because as of now, you can consider yourself warned. We'll get you back for this. I don't know how, and I don't know when. But when we do, it'll be big. Really big. And—"

"Tiffany, calm down," Gail said. "It's obvious someone played a practical joke on you, and I'm sorry for that. I'm sorry *some* people never learn.

But don't let it ruin your trip." Gail turned to Stephanie and held out her hand. "Camera, please."

"What?" Stephanie gripped the camera tightly.

"I'm going to hold on to your camera," Gail said. "Till we get to the bottom of this."

"But I'm keeping a journal, with photos," Stephanie argued. "I need pictures! And it's my dad's camera. He made me promise I'd take really, really good care of it. I can't let it out of my sight."

Gail was still standing with her hand extended toward the camera. "I'll be very careful with it. And when you've proved you're not causing—or even enjoying—all these mishaps, I'll be happy to return it."

"Whatever happened to 'innocent until proven guilty'?" Stephanie muttered.

"Stephanie," Gail warned.

Stephanie let out a sigh and handed her camera to Gail. Great. *Cool Adventure* would never publish her journal without photographs.

"Tough break," Darcy commented as they walked away from the shower area. Anna, Kayla, and Allie had all run over when they heard Tiffany scream.

"This is so weird." Stephanie turned to her

friends. "Who do you think is responsible for all these practical jokes on the Flamingoes?"

"I don't know, but they should get a medal!" Anna laughed. "Turning Tiffany's shower green was brilliant."

"I couldn't have done any better myself," Darcy said.

Allie giggled. "It was so hard to take Tiffany seriously. Standing there with green goo on her head, threatening you . . ."

"She looked like Godzilla junior!" Kayla snickered.

"You guys! I can't believe you think it was funny." Stephanie frowned. "I got in trouble with Gail again. She took away my camera."

Darcy shrugged. "You'll get it back. Anyway, wasn't it worth losing your camera for? At least she didn't take your film out. Ooh, I can't wait until you get that roll developed. We're talking serious blackmail material."

"Darcy! You sound like you're enjoying this!" Stephanie cried.

Darcy stared at Stephanie as if she were crazy. "Well, why *wouldn't* I?"

"Because we promised we'd leave the Flamingoes alone this summer," Stephanie said. "And *we* didn't do anything. But there's something I don't get. Why would anyone *else* want to ruin Tiffany's hair?''

"Well, she's pretty obnoxious," Allie began. "It wouldn't take long for her to get on someone's nerves."

"No kidding," Kayla said. "Within five seconds of meeting me, she was already rude!"

"Okay, so she's not going to win any niceness contests," Stephanie said. "But the only people who might really hold something against her are standing right here."

Darcy stared at Stephanie. "Are you actually accusing us?"

Stephanie felt a twinge of guilt. She didn't *want* to accuse her friends.

"We didn't have anything to do with what just happened," Anna said calmly.

"Really? I mean, I believe you." *I guess*, Stephanie thought. "But what about last night?" She looked at Darcy.

"I didn't put those frogs in Cynthia's sleeping bag," Darcy replied. "And I can't believe you'd think I *would*."

"I don't want to think that," Stephanie said. "I really don't. But I know you want to win our bet. So maybe you're pulling these pranks in order to stir up trouble between me and the Flamingoes."

Darcy looked annoyed. "Steph, I told you I'd

go along with your peace plan," she said. "And maybe I can see why you're suspicious, but I haven't broken my promise. I'm sure no one else has, either."

"I believe you," Stephanie said. "Really." *At least, I'm trying to*, she thought. *Even though I can't think of any other explanation for what's going on!*

"Okay, everyone—welcome to the Yampa River!" Steve Preston, one of the counselors, announced the next morning. He stood on a rock by the river, Gail beside him.

Stephanie walked over to the river's edge. They'd driven the whole day before and into the night to reach the put-in point, in northern Colorado. She craned her neck to see the top of the river canyon. Spectacular red cliff walls towered above them. Eagles soared through the bright blue sky.

"We'll start here and end in northern Utah in three days, at Dinosaur National Park," Steve said. "The river starts off fairly calm, which will give you a chance to get used to being in a raft. You'll learn how to paddle as a team, and get comfortable. Then we'll hit some of the more intense water."

"White water—right? Rapids!" Bruce cried.

"Exactly," Steve said.

Stephanie walked over to look at the blue and yellow rafts. They were large, and made of thick rubber.

"Rapids are rated according to how difficult they are to navigate," Steve continued. "They're put into categories called classes, which range from one to six. Class One rapids are very easy. Class Two are for novices. That's where we'll start out. Along the way, we'll also encounter Class Three and Four rapids. A few of the more difficult areas on this river are Whirlpool Canyon and Warm Springs. They will be our first Super Summer Adventure Super Challenge. You can look forward to those!" Steve grinned.

"Whirlpool Canyon!" Darcy came up beside Stephanie to check out the rafts. "Now, *that* sounds like fun."

"Definitely," Stephanie agreed. She couldn't wait to get on the water.

"Now for a short safety talk before we start out," Steve continued. "You'll see we have life jackets and helmets for all of you. You need to wear those whenever we're on the river."

"And you know what that means," Kayla said. "Helmet hair."

Everyone standing around her laughed.

"Now, if you'll all look at this boat right here." Steve and Gail lifted a raft and stood it on end.

"You'll sit here, on the outside edge of the raft. You can press your leg against the thwarts—these tubes that go across—to keep your balance. Tuck your feet underneath to keep from falling out. The number-one rule of rafting is, stay in the boat! No matter what!"

"Rescues are difficult and dangerous," Gail said. "So try to stay in your raft even when giant waves hit it. We can't emphasize that enough."

"Rapids can easily flip a boat." Steve made a turning motion with his hands. "And when they do, it's a challenge to swim with the current working against you. As we raft today, we'll tell you more about what to do in case of emergency. Basically, what I want to get across is that you can't take rafting lightly. You have to focus at all times. You need to follow our directions *exactly*. Got it?"

He looked at the crowd of campers. "All right, then. I have a list here of who should be in which raft. Listen up for your name!"

Stephanie crossed her fingers behind her back as Steve started calling out names. She knew there would be five or six campers in each raft, and she wanted to be in the same raft as her friends. But she also really wanted to raft with Tim. No one was looking forward to the adventure more than he was, so it would be a blast to paddle with him.

"Gail is the counselor on the next raft. And join-
ing Gail are"—Steve consulted his list—"Allie,
Darcy, Stephanie, Bruce, Roberta, and Tim. Hop
on!"

Stephanie couldn't believe how lucky she was.
Not only would she get to raft with a couple of
her best friends, but with Tim, too. And no
Flamingoes.

This rafting trip was off to an awesome start!

Darcy looked at Stephanie and smiled. "Yes!
We're together!"

"Isn't it great?" Stephanie said.

As she put on her helmet, Tim walked over.

"Let's sit in the front," he said to Stephanie.
"Are you up for getting good and wet?"

"Definitely," Stephanie told him, thrilled that
he wanted to sit with her. She clipped the strap
on her helmet to fasten it. "Do you think we'll
get splashed?'

"Drenched," Tim said. "Isn't that the point?"
He laughed.

"Allie, why don't you sit back here across from
me," Darcy said. "I heard that the paddlers in
front have to do *all* the work."

"No problem. We *want* to work. Right, Stephanie?" Tim smiled as he stepped into the raft and
sat down beside her.

"Definitely!" Stephanie said. "Besides, I want to be the first to see *everything.*"

"Roberta, you can sit in the middle, across from Bruce," Gail instructed. She guided the raft into the water as soon as the final two campers were on it.

Stephanie glanced over her shoulder. She already knew Bruce from all the obnoxious jokes he'd made since the trip began. Roberta was tall, with auburn hair that fell down her back in a long braid.

"Is everyone ready?" Gail asked. "Then we're off!" She stepped into the raft and it started floating along with the current. "We'll drift for a while. Then I'll run through some paddling commands," Gail said.

"Isn't this awesome?" Tim asked Stephanie. "We're finally on the river!"

Stephanie nodded. She was enjoying the gentle bobbing of the raft in the water. In a few minutes, they'd be hitting their first white water. She could hardly wait! But she didn't want to say all that to Tim. She didn't want to talk his ear off.

"Have you ever been rafting before?" Tim asked.

"No," Stephanie said.

"Canoeing?"

Stephanie nodded. "Yes." Behind her, she could

hear Allie and Darcy talking. Gail was explaining to Bruce and Roberta how she steered the boat.

"Canoes are great. I love the way they glide smoothly through the water," Tim said. "How about sailing? Do you like sailing?"

"I spent almost all last summer sailing, actually," Stephanie told him.

"Really? You must be good at it," Tim said.

"I'm okay," Stephanie said shyly. She could sense that Tim was watching her.

"Is something wrong?" he asked. "You've been so quiet today. Is everything okay? Or am I asking too many questions and getting on your nerves?"

"No," Stephanie blurted out. "Not at all. I think it's just that I'm kind of distracted. I've never been in a raft before. And I keep looking at all the incredible canyon scenery." *And trying not to come on too strong and push you away*, she added silently to herself.

"Forward paddle!" Gail called out the first paddling command. Stephanie dipped her paddle in the water, and the raft shot forward.

"Are you ready for the ride of your life?" Tim gave Stephanie a big smile. His muscles flexed as he paddled with strong, sure strokes.

Wow, he's an incredible athlete, Stephanie thought.

They rounded a bend in the river and entered

a red-walled canyon. There were a few rafts ahead of them, and a few behind.

"Stephanie, check out that canyon wall. See the way it sort of curves at the top?" Tim asked. "And look at that fantastic rock formation on the top of it. It looks almost like a little tower."

Stephanie peered around, looking for the wall.

"Over there—behind me!" Tim said.

Stephanie leaned forward to see what he was talking about. She spotted the curved wall, and then the rocks on top. "It seems ancient," she commented. "Like an altar of some kind. Or maybe a lookout post, so they could see who was coming down the river."

Tim turned to her. "I bet you're right. Maybe we could do some exploring together—you know, separate from the group." He looked excitedly at Stephanie, and their eyes met.

Her heart lurched. "That would be . . . great," she said breathlessly. *That would be incredible, fantastic, awesome,* she thought as she smiled at Tim. She could see them now: looking for arrowheads and artifacts in the moonlight, holding hands as they hopped over a small stream, gazing at constellations, kissing. . . .

She closed her eyes, picturing the perfect romantic moment.

"Stephanie!" someone screeched. "Watch out!"

CHAPTER

8

◆ ◂ ▪ ◆

Whaa—?

Startled, Stephanie opened her eyes. A huge tree limb jutted out over the river. It was aimed right at her head! She held her arms in front of her face and started to duck.

"Hold on—I've got you!" Tim grabbed hold of Stephanie's shoulders and yanked her back. She tumbled into the bottom of the raft.

A small branch brushed Stephanie's arm, but the big limb missed her head.

"Great save, Tim!" Cynthia called from the raft beside theirs. "Wow, you've got quick reflexes."

"Yeah, you sure do," Stephanie told Tim. She scrambled back up onto the tube. "I'd be in the river now if it weren't for you. With a very big bump on my head," she added.

"No problem," Tim said. "You'd do the same for me, right?"

In a heartbeat, Stephanie thought. "Of course," she said, smiling. She wanted to thank him more, but she stopped herself. Tim didn't like girls who came on too strong.

"Tim, did you ever play racquetball?" Cynthia called.

"Lots of times. Why?" Tim replied.

"Because it's the same kind of quick reflex you use in that game," Cynthia said.

"You know what? You're right," Tim said with a laugh.

Since when does Cynthia play racquetball? Stephanie fumed. The last Stephanie knew, she didn't play any sport that might involve her breaking a perfectly manicured pink fingernail.

"Do you play?" Tim asked.

Ah-ha! Stephanie thought. *Now we'll find out the truth.*

"A little. But I like tennis better," Cynthia answered. "I played on the school team last year. I was ranked first in singles."

Stephanie felt confused. Maybe Cynthia really was an athlete. That meant that she and Tim actually did have something in common.

Quit worrying about Cynthia, Stephanie told herself. She stared straight ahead at the river. *Focus on yourself.* Besides, Tim would never go for someone as vain, as artificial, as loud as Cynthia—no matter how good she was in sports. Would he?

She quickly stole a glance at Tim. She wondered if there was any way she could paddle so their raft would drift away from Cynthia's.

It wouldn't do any good, Stephanie knew and sighed. She couldn't really get away from Cynthia. They were stuck with each other for a whole month.

I've got to put up with Cynthia. Otherwise Darcy will win the bet.

But how can I be nice to someone who wants to steal the boy of my dreams?

"I can't believe how hungry I was. And that was only an afternoon of rafting!" Anna popped the last bite of a turkey dog into her mouth. They were camping that night in a tiny area by the riverbank barely large enough for all their tents. The counselors had assigned a group of campers to cook dinner: hot dogs, turkey dogs, and campfire biscuits.

"I was starving, too," Darcy said. "But I might have eaten a few too many of those biscuits."

"You'll need your strength for tomorrow,"

Stephanie told her brightly. She was still pumped from the day on the river. They went through three areas of white water, and every muscle in her body ached. She couldn't wait to get out on the river to do it again.

"I think we'll all need lots of strength for tomorrow." Tim smiled at Stephanie as he grabbed another biscuit. "We're supposed to hit some Class Three rapids."

Cynthia sat down beside him on a log. "I hope we'll be in different boats tomorrow. Then maybe we can paddle together," she told Tim.

"That would be cool," Tim said. "Then we wouldn't have to yell across the river when we wanted to talk."

Stephanie was in the middle of taking a bite, and she nearly choked on her hot dog. *No*, she thought desperately. *Don't tell me this goes both ways. Don't tell me Tim likes her, too!*

Stephanie decided the only thing she could do was join the conversation. "Yeah, you guys were kind of . . . loud," she said.

"So? Is there some sort of noise law for the river?" Cynthia joked. "No sirens, no car alarms, no talking—"

"All I meant," Stephanie said, "was that all the shouting kind of, uh, distracted me. From appreciating nature."

"Nature. You mean that branch that almost knocked you overboard?" Cynthia giggled.

Stephanie bit her lip. There were a thousand things she wanted to say back—but she couldn't. She had said she wouldn't let the Flamingoes get to her. But she hadn't known it was going to be so hard!

Lucky for her, Tim was sitting right there to keep her from saying something she'd regret. Unfortunately, he was still sitting next to Cynthia, too.

Molly passed a plate to Darah. "Care for a s'more?"

Stephanie stared at the stack of graham cracker, chocolate, and toasted marshmallow sandwiches. Her mouth was practically watering!

"Don't you guys *love* these?" Darah asked as she took one.

"I do," Cynthia said. She lifted one off the plate and handed it to Tim. "One for you, one for me—"

"Thanks." Tim took a bite of the graham cracker. His mouth was covered in marshmallow.

Cynthia pointed at him and giggled. "You have marshmallow mouth!"

"Oh, yeah? Well, what do you think *you* have?" Tim replied. "Is that a new lipstick color? Marshmallow white?"

Cynthia laughed. "Tim, you're so funny. I'm so glad you're on this trip! It would be totally dull without you."

Stephanie munched a s'more and stared into the campfire. She didn't know how much more of this she could take. *Mind over Flamingoes*, she repeated to herself. *Mind over Flamingoes*.

But what she really felt like saying was "Move over, Flamingoes. And leave me and Tim alone!"

Today was weird. Things aren't going exactly the way I wanted. Cynthia and Tim are best friends all of a sudden.

Stephanie was too tired to write any more. She dropped her pen and laid her journal on her stomach. *I wish Gail would give me back my camera*, she thought as she stretched out and closed her eyes. *What good is a travel journal without pictures?*

She was just drifting off to sleep when she heard a loud shriek outside her tent. Stephanie sat bolt upright in her sleeping bag.

Kayla opened her eyes slowly. "Not Cynthia again?"

"I hope not," Stephanie mumbled. She unzipped the flap and poked her head out.

"*Bear!*" Mikki stood in the center of the campsite, screaming. "I saw a bear right there! It walked right past my tent!"

"What did?" Cynthia asked. She walked over to Mikki and looked around.

"A bear!" Mikki shrieked.

"You're kidding," Darah said. By now everyone was peering out of their tents.

"I wish I were! Oh, my gosh, it was huge! Ask Jenny. She saw the shadow go by our tent, too," Mikki said, out of breath.

"Mikki, don't get hysterical. You might have thought you saw a bear, but the chances of running into one up here are very slim," Molly said, soothing her.

"That bear wasn't slim. It was gigantic!" Mikki exclaimed. "Its feet were this big." She held her hands about three feet apart. "What if it's a grizzly?"

"There aren't any grizzlies around here," Gail said calmly. "There are black bears, but we packed all the food away. Bears show up only when there's food. There's nothing here to tempt them."

"Except me," Mikki protested. "That bear could feed on us campers for days. You should have seen how huge it was!"

"Mikki, please, you need to calm down," Gail said. "Bears don't attack humans unless they're

73

provoked. Any idea you have about a bear stalking us comes from the movies, not real life."

"Hmm," Mikki grumbled. "Well, where do you think they *got* the ideas for the movies? Real life!"

"Come on." Molly put an arm around Mikki's shoulders. "I'll walk you back to your tent, and then I'll stand guard outside tonight, just to make sure."

"And I'll patrol the other tents, watching for anything unusual," Gail promised. "We'll make sure this is a bear-free zone."

"It's possible your mind was playing tricks on you." Molly guided Mikki away from the clearing. "You know how it is when you're tired. You probably saw pine needles, not hair. Don't worry," Molly told her. "Whatever it was, we'll figure it out."

Stephanie shivered at the thought of a bear in the campsite. She didn't know whether to feel excited—or scared. She felt very far from San Francisco.

Tim walked over to Stephanie. "Wow. Do you really think a bear was here?"

"A bear? No." Then Stephanie reconsidered. "Well, maybe. It happens, right?"

"Once in a while, I guess. I wouldn't want to run into a bear up close. But I'd love to see one this summer," Tim said. "While we're up here in the mountains and all."

"Me, too, as long as it's from a distance. Definitely!" Stephanie said with a laugh.

"Sure. Binoculars could come in handy for bear sightings," Tim agreed. "Then again, so could the zoo. One of my favorite places. Hey, maybe when we get back home, we could go sometime."

Stephanie couldn't believe it. Tim had just asked her out! They had a date for August, and it was only June.

"Absolutely," Stephanie replied. "I'd like that."

Tim took a step closer. The moonlight cast a shadow across his face.

This is so romantic! Stephanie thought. Standing outside with the moon, a soft breeze, and Tim . . . Stephanie moved forward and reached for Tim's hand.

A twig crunched loudly, and Cynthia appeared as if out of nowhere. "Tim! Did you hear the plan?"

"Uh, plan? What plan?" Tim asked. He took a step back from Stephanie.

The plan to ruin the most romantic moment of my life, Stephanie thought as she glared helplessly at Cynthia.

"Some of the guys are talking about waiting up for the bear. When it comes, they're going to chase it and try to scare it away," Cynthia said. "Naturally, Mikki's *not* into the idea."

"She's still pretty freaked out, huh?" Tim asked.

"Well, yeah, she is. Who wouldn't be?" Cynthia said. "Of course, you probably wouldn't be. You'd probably run out of your tent and say hi."

Tim laughed. "Not likely. I do value my life. But thanks for believing in me."

Stephanie stared at Tim. He didn't seem to mind when Cynthia came on strong. But Stephanie minded. A lot. The night had been a total disaster as far as she and Tim were concerned.

"Excuse me," she said stiffly. "I need to get a drink of water." While Cynthia and Tim kept talking, she slipped down to the edge of the river. The group in her boat had stashed bottles of drinking water inside a mesh bag anchored by a rock.

Stephanie found her bottle and lifted it to her lips. The icy cold water was so refreshing. She stood by the river and listened to the water rush past. She began to calm down. Being out in the wilderness at night was so peaceful, she thought.

Stephanie capped her bottle and put it back in the mesh bag. Then she turned to walk back up toward the circle of tents. She clicked her flashlight on and shined it back and forth on the narrow trail. She didn't want to trip on any exposed tree roots.

Suddenly her flashlight beam swept over something in the undergrowth.

Something brown and hairy.

She saw huge claws reaching out toward her.

"Ack!" Stephanie screamed. "Bear!"

CHAPTER
9

♦ ◂ ◾ ♦

Stephanie's body froze. It was too late to run from the bear, too late to call for help. . . . She expected to see a huge brown shape come crashing out of the bushes at any moment.

Then she realized her flashlight was shining on nothing but the dark night air. There was no bear in front of her!

She aimed the beam at the ground again. The giant foot was still there. It hadn't moved an inch.

"What's going on?" Stephanie stepped forward and poked the furry object with her toe.

It flipped over. And she saw a rubber sole on the bottom.

"It's a slipper!" She heaved a sigh of relief and lifted the slipper from the ground.

"We heard you scream. What's wrong?" Steve asked. He and a group of campers rushed toward her.

"I heard you say *bear.* Did you see the bear?" Mikki asked. She was out of breath from running after the others.

"It's no bear, Mikki. I promise." Stephanie grinned.

"Then why did you yell *bear?* This isn't funny," Mikki said. "Quit teasing me and tell me what's going on!"

"I would if I could, but I don't know what's going on, exactly. But if I had to guess, I'd say . . . a practical joke?" Stephanie held up the furry slipper.

Mikki gasped. "What? It's a lousy slipper?"

"Where did you get that?" Gail asked.

"I found it on the ground," Stephanie said. "Just a minute ago."

Gail frowned. "Is that the bear foot you saw, Mikki?"

Mikki nodded.

"I thought you said you saw a huge bear," Gail went on. "Didn't you mention the giant shadow?"

"I did see a shadow," Mikki insisted. She reddened in embarrassment. "Just not so huge, maybe."

"Hmm. Well, someone was obviously wearing

this slipper to try to scare you. So the question is, who?" Gail surveyed the crowd of campers. Then she turned back to Stephanie. "Well?"

"Well, what?" Stephanie asked, startled. "I don't know who did it. I came down here for a drink of water. That's when I saw it."

Gail shone a flashlight on the area where the slipper had been. "There are footsteps leading away. Stephanie, are you sure this is the first time you've been here this evening?"

Stephanie couldn't restrain her anger any longer. "I didn't have anything to do with the slipper. I was asleep when Mikki thought she saw the bear. Wasn't I, Kayla?"

Kayla nodded. "She was in the tent with me."

"Well, we'll see," Gail said. "Now, everyone, go back to bed. It's late." She turned on her heel and walked back up the hill.

"I have a new name for Gail," Darcy suggested. "How about Sergeant Gail?"

"No—General Gail!" Allie giggled.

"Perfect," Anna agreed.

"So, Stephanie. How did you manage to sneak out of the tent while Kayla was asleep? And where in the world did you get that horrible slipper?" Darcy asked.

Stephanie couldn't believe her ears. "What?"

"Come on, Steph! You were caught red-handed," Anna said. "Did you bring the slipper from home? Was it left over from a Halloween costume or something?"

"You guys! I never saw that slipper before." Stephanie felt totally frustrated. "I wasn't behind this. Just like I wasn't behind any of the other pranks being played on the Flamingoes."

"If you say so . . ." Darcy didn't sound convinced.

"Darcy, it's not me," Stephanie argued. "How could you think I'd be involved?"

"Call me crazy. But a few days ago you were the one stealing their luggage," Darcy said. "Maybe I don't believe in overnight transformations, okay?"

"Well, you'd better start. I trust you guys, don't I?" Stephanie asked.

"I don't know. Do you?" Darcy replied.

"Of course," Stephanie said. At least, she was trying to. "But if you guys didn't scare Mikki, and I didn't scare Mikki, who did?" she asked.

"Beats me. None of this makes any sense," Anna said. "I'm going to quit trying to figure it out and go back to bed."

"Me, too," Allie chimed in.

Stephanie headed back to her tent with Kayla. Anna was right. It didn't make sense. Unless one of them was doing the pranks on her own, and keeping it a secret from everyone else.

She wanted to be able to trust her friends. She just didn't know if she could.

"Listen up," Molly announced after breakfast the next day. "Gail has the lists of who's in which raft. She'll be coming around to find you. We decided to change things around again," Molly said. "Give people a chance to visit and get to know new people."

"Great," Allie said sarcastically. "Just the way we change in the vans."

"Hey, that's turned out okay, hasn't it?" Stephanie reminded her as campers milled around, directed by Gail.

"Sure—for *you* and your love life," Allie teased.

"Shh! Here comes Gail," Stephanie warned.

"Allie, you're in Steve's raft, right over there." Gail pointed with her pen. "And, Stephanie— you're in this raft today." She turned to a raft just to her left. "With me."

"What? But I—" Stephanie glanced at Tim. He was sitting on a raft at the other end of the line. Then she saw Cynthia get into the same raft!

"Jenny and Mikki, you're also in with me and Stephanie," Gail said.

Stephanie couldn't believe her bad luck! Gail, Jenny, and Mikki?

Stay calm, Stephanie told herself. Stay serene. Everything will work out.

"And Bruce and Kevin," Gail continued. "That should be everyone. . . ."

"Okay. Grab your gear, people—it's time to shove off!" Steve yelled. "Get ready for another awesome day on the river!"

"I'll see you later," Allie said. "Good luck."

"Thanks," Stephanie said, climbing into her raft. "I think I'm going to need it!"

Nothing like being the last ones in, Stephanie thought as her raft cruised toward the riverbank a few hours later. All the other rafts were already tied to trees or beached.

"Okay, Stephanie, bring us in!" Gail directed from the stern.

"Me?" Stephanie asked. "But—"

"I'll steer, but I want you to help," Gail said. "Since you've been doing such a good job paddling, you can call out the strokes until we hit shore. Just tell everyone which way to paddle."

"Okay," Stephanie said. At least she'd impressed Gail by her devoted paddling.

Stephanie looked over the raft for a moment. Then she decided what they should do.

"All right, Mikki and Jenny, you guys keep paddling the way you are," Stephanie said. The two Flamingoes were sitting on the right side of the boat, chatting and gazing up at the hot sun.

"Kevin, Bruce—when we get up to that tree, I want you to start paddling as hard as you can. You'll be downstream, and you'll need to push hard to bring us onto shore," Stephanie told them.

She saw Bruce and Kevin whisper to each other. Bruce then observed Stephanie looking at him, and he straightened up and gave her a quick salute.

"Ready and . . . go!" she commanded as they passed the tree.

Bruce's and Kevin's paddles churned through the water.

"Stroke," Stephanie called out. "Stroke!"

"Harder," Gail said. "Harder or we won't make it!"

Stephanie jumped behind Kevin and started paddling, too. With the strength of four paddlers, they managed to head fairly straight. But as they got close to the shore, the current started spinning the raft away from the bank. Stephanie had to move fast!

She leapt to the right side of the raft, to Jenny and Mikki's side. Only the bottom of the boat was slick, and her sandal slipped. She crashed into Jenny, who was just stepping out of the raft.

Stephanie watched in horror as Jenny fell overboard.

"Oh, no," Stephanie moaned. Jenny sank under the water and splashed about in the swift current. When she came up again, she was sputtering.

"Grab my hand," Stephanie said. She leaned over the side and pulled Jenny up as the others beached the raft. "I'm so sorry," she apologized. "There was something slippery on the raft."

"Yeah, you!" Jenny said. She pushed strands of dripping wet hair off her face. "What a rotten trick that was!"

"It wasn't a trick!" Stephanie cried. "Honest. I think somebody dropped some sunscreen or baby oil on the raft."

"Maybe *somebody* did. *You!*" Mikki got out of the raft and helped Jenny up the bank.

"It was a mistake!" Stephanie said. "I promise!" She turned around to face Gail. "You believe me, don't you? You can feel that gunk on the rubber. You know I was trying to land the raft, not knock Jenny into the river."

Gail shook her head. "Actually, I *don't* know about you at all, Stephanie." She gave Stephanie a hard look. "If these pranks keep up, I don't even know if you'll be allowed to stay on the trip." Then she got out and walked up to talk to the other counselors.

Stephanie couldn't believe her bad luck. Instead of making things better with Gail, she had just made them ten times worse. There were more than three weeks left to her Super Summer Adventure.

Now Stephanie didn't even know if she'd make it through the next day!

CHAPTER
10

◆ ◂ ◗ ◆

"Sorry you got in trouble with Gail," Bruce said as he and Stephanie tied up their raft.

Stephanie sighed as she took off her wet sandals. "Which time are you talking about?"

"Just now, when we came in on the raft." Bruce placed the paddles in the center of the boat. "I bet Jenny or Mikki dripped their suntan lotion onto the raft. That's why you slipped. Sorry."

"That's okay," Stephanie told him. "No big deal." At least, unless you considered having a counselor on your case a big deal.

"And like last night, with the bear slipper," Bruce said. "Did you pull that off like she thought?"

Stephanie shook her head. "No way. I just

found the slipper lying on the ground. But Gail's convinced I'm up to no good, so she assumed I'd pulled the prank. I didn't, though."

"Oh." Bruce shrugged. "Well, it sure seems like a lot of weird stuff has been happening. And it keeps happening to that one group of girls. I wonder why."

"Actually, I think I know why—" Stephanie hesitated. "I probably shouldn't say anything. Never mind."

"No, wait—what were you going to say?" Bruce asked. "Because to be honest, I find the whole thing kind of fascinating."

"You do?" Stephanie asked.

"Sure. It's like something out of a movie," Bruce said. "The pretty but obnoxious girls get what's coming to them."

"Well, if anyone deserves it, it's them," Stephanie said. "And that's why I think my friends have something to do with what's been happening."

"Your friends? Like Darcy?" Bruce asked. "And Allie?"

Stephanie nodded. "Exactly. I just can't believe they're not involved. I don't have any proof or anything. But if anyone has a reason to do it, they're the ones."

"Really? Why?" Bruce prodded.

"This might sound dumb, but Darah and her friends have been our worst enemies for a really long time," Stephanie explained. "We've had this sort of feud between us. But I decided that this summer, I'd ignore them. Forget the whole thing. And I thought my friends wanted to go along with me. At least they all promised they did."

"But now you think they bailed on you?" Bruce asked.

"Yeah. I do," Stephanie said. "And if they are behind this, we'll get kicked off the trip. I know Gail can't wait to send me home!"

"Nah," Bruce said. He shook his head. "She wouldn't do that. She's all talk. We all paid to be on this trip, and you'd have to do something pretty drastic to be forced to leave. So don't worry about that."

"Okay, I'll try not to. Thanks," Stephanie told him. "I feel kind of bad for accusing my friends like I just did."

"Hey, you said it yourself. Nothing else makes sense," Bruce argued. "They're the ones with the motive."

"I'm not sure." Stephanie frowned. "Well, thanks for listening."

"Anytime." Bruce shrugged. "Well, see you later."

"Bye!" Stephanie called. She felt confused.

Bruce was so obnoxious when his friends were around. After he'd laughed at her for having that "nerd" sign taped to her back, Stephanie had never imagined having a real conversation with him.

I guess this is what this trip is all about, Stephanie thought. *Meeting new people and making new friends—like Bruce.*

After dinner Stephanie joined all the other campers sitting around the campfire. Some people were sipping hot chocolate, while others roasted marshmallows over the glowing embers.

"So, I wonder if we'll see any more bears tonight," Tiffany said.

"I doubt it," Darah said. She took a pocket knife out of her khaki shorts to cut an apple into quarters. Stephanie couldn't believe it—even her knife was pink. It matched her sweatshirt perfectly. "Considering bears need two feet to walk around and Gail has one of them."

"You know what's really weird? Someone sitting around this fire probably pulled that stunt," Jenny said. "And it's horrible to think there are people in this group who can't be trusted."

"How could you even live with yourself?" Tiffany wondered.

"Get over it!" Darcy said. "Nobody got hurt or anything. Actually, it was kind of funny."

"Oh, yeah. It was hilarious," Mikki grumbled. "You weren't *there*, okay?"

"Nobody was there," Darah said. "And that's what doesn't make sense. Didn't anyone else hear something? Doesn't anyone have any evidence?"

"Actually . . ." Bruce glanced across the fire at Stephanie. "Stephanie told me that she might know who did it."

"What?" Stephanie demanded. "I never said—"

"So you *were* responsible!" Cynthia shouted.

"No, it isn't her! It's *them*." Bruce pointed at Darcy, Anna, Kayla, and Allie. "Stephanie even has proof that they've been involved in all the pranks!"

"No! I never said that," Stephanie protested.

"Well? Did you guys do it?" Bruce asked them.

"No!" Darcy's voice rang out almost as loudly as Kayla's as they both denied the accusation.

Allie stared at Stephanie. Her eyes were blazing with anger. "We haven't done a thing. How could you say something like that about us?"

"I never said you did it," Stephanie pleaded.

"Well, yeah, you kind of *did*," Bruce corrected her.

So much for confiding in so-called new friends! Stephanie thought. "All I said was that it sort of would make sense if you guys pulled the pranks, but I said I didn't have any proof."

"So now you're *looking* for proof?" Darcy asked. "Oh, that's nice. Gathering evidence on your best friends?"

"Excuse me, Darcy. *Best friends* doesn't seem to apply here," Anna said coldly. "More like ex— best friends."

"What? No!" Stephanie cried. "I'm sorry. I didn't really think that you guys would do this, I just—"

"You just decided to say it? In front of everyone?" Anna asked. "Well, thanks for being so *thoughtful*. Really!"

"Come on, you guys. Let's go. I want to talk in private." Darcy got to her feet.

One by one, Kayla, Anna, and Allie stood up, too. The four of them disappeared behind a clump of trees.

"Nice going, Stephanie," Darah said. "You know, it's probably not too late."

Stephanie frowned. "To make it up to them?" she muttered.

"No." Darah giggled. "To tell the counselors you want to go home for the rest of the summer! Maybe you can still get a refund."

Stephanie leapt up and stormed over to where

Bruce was standing with his friends. "Bruce! How could you do that to me?" she demanded.

"I didn't mean to get you in trouble. It just slipped out," Bruce said.

"Well, don't you think before you speak?" Stephanie said.

"Look, don't get all angry at me," Bruce said. "I was only repeating what you told me."

"In confidence," Stephanie said. "I didn't expect you to tell the entire group."

"Stephanie, look, I didn't mean to make trouble. I said I was sorry. What else can I do?" Bruce held up his hands.

"Nothing," Stephanie grumbled. "You've done enough!"

As mad as she was at Bruce, Stephanie knew she was partly responsible for what had happened. She shouldn't have confided in Bruce. She barely knew him. What was more, she'd believed everything she said—at the time, anyway.

Now she wasn't sure what to think. All she knew was that she had made her best friends mad at her.

Stephanie went back to her tent to look for Kayla. But Kayla wasn't there. She was probably still out talking with Anna, Darcy, and Allie— about Stephanie.

And she'd have every right to, Stephanie

thought as she hung her flashlight from the tent ceiling. She took out her journal and started writing.

What if Darcy and everyone else really didn't have anything to do with the Flamingo pranks? What if they're innocent? They'll never forgive me!

We all came on this trip to have a good time together. Now they're not talking to me—all because I don't trust them.

Oh, no. What did I just do?

CHAPTER
11

◆ ◀ ◣ ◆

"Kayla? Do you want me to take down the tent?" Stephanie asked the next morning.

Kayla didn't reply. She was stuffing her mummy-shaped sleeping bag into its sack.

Kayla hadn't said a word to Stephanie all night. She'd sneaked in late, after Stephanie was asleep. She hadn't even returned Stephanie's apologetic "good morning." Kayla obviously didn't plan on speaking to Stephanie today, either.

They can't hold a grudge forever, can they? Stephanie wondered as she folded the ground cloth. She rolled it up with the tent and stuffed them into the carrying bag. Then she went over to one of the gear rafts. Darcy and Anna were standing beside it, drinking bottled water.

Stephanie walked up to them. She felt very self-conscious. "Hi," she said. "Getting ready for the rapids?"

Anna glanced at her with a blank expression. Darcy didn't even turn around.

"I'm sorry," she ventured. "About last night. I didn't know Bruce was going to say anything."

"I think I've had enough water. How about you?" Darcy asked.

"I'm all set," Anna said.

Stephanie watched as Anna and Darcy walked off. Hadn't they heard her apology, or didn't they care? She shoved her backpack into the raft and tied a strap down to secure it. When she turned around, she saw Allie by the river's edge putting on her sandals.

"Allie!" Stephanie hurried over to her. "How are you?"

"Fine," Allie said curtly. She fastened one of her Velcro sandal straps.

Stephanie crouched in front of her. "You're not still mad at me, are you?" she asked.

"Well, actually, yeah. I am," Allie admitted. "I can't believe you'd try to make us look bad in front of everyone—especially the Flamingoes!"

"But I didn't plan to do that," Stephanie tried to explain. "It was an accident. Bruce and I were talking about stuff that happened in the raft with Gail and—"

Allie got to her feet. "I don't really care how it happened. The fact is that you humiliated us. And it's going to take more than a little apology to make it up to us. Because you don't trust us, Stephanie E veryone thinks we're the bad guys now. And we're *not*." Allie stared angrily at Stephanie for a second, then turned and ran up the hill.

Stephanie watched her go. How did everything go so wrong?

Tim will understand, she thought. *He'll know that I didn't mean for any of this to happen.*

Stephanie found Tim helping pack up the breakfast supplies. "Hey, Tim. Almost done?" she asked.

"All done!" He cinched the bag that held stacking saucepans. "Why?"

"I was wondering. Do you want to go for a short hike while everyone else gets ready?" Stephanie asked. "Maybe climb up the canyon a little ways, see what we can find?" She wanted to talk to Tim about her problem with her friends. Maybe he'd know what she should do.

"Well . . ." Tim hesitated.

"Please?" Stephanie begged. "We have almost half an hour before we shove off."

Tim looked at her for a second. "Yeah. Okay. I wanted to talk to you, anyway."

Stephanie felt a flutter of excitement. She hadn't had a chance to be alone with him since the night Mikki thought she saw the bear. Whenever Tim was around, Cynthia always seemed to show up.

Tim finished packing the dishes and turned them over to a counselor to stow in one of the gear rafts. Then he stood up and brushed off his hands. "Let's go."

"So, want to head up those rocks?" Stephanie asked. "I bet we'd have a great view of the river."

Tim shrugged. "Sounds good." He followed her up the steep, rocky cliff. A small path had been worn into the rock by visitors over the years.

When they reached the top, Stephanie could see for miles. The frothy brown river wound into the misty distance. She could see patches of swirling water and what looked like small waterfalls.

"Looks like we'll be hitting real rapids right ahead of us," she said. "I can't *wait* to see those walls of water Gail keeps talking about."

"Yeah, neither can I. Hey, you want to sit down for a second?" Tim asked.

"Sure. Look at this fabulous view!" Stephanie perched on a rock beside Tim. "The canyon walls are streaked black and white, like a tiger's stripes."

She paused. "Listen, Tim, I was wondering . . ."

"Stephanie, I don't know how to say this, so I'm just going to take a stab at it," Tim interrupted her.

What's this all about? Stephanie wondered.

"What's going on with you?" he asked. His blue eyes looked directly into Stephanie's.

"What do you mean?" Stephanie asked, puzzled.

"I feel like you're up to something—all the time. And I have no idea what it is, or why you're doing it," Tim said.

"Up to what?" Stephanie said. "I'm not responsible for those practical jokes—why won't anyone believe me?"

"I'm not talking about the stupid pranks!" Tim exclaimed. "I'm talking about the way you are with people."

"People?" Stephanie repeated. She had no idea what he was talking about. "Tell me you don't mean Cynthia and the rest of the Flamingoes. Because I've been nothing but nice to them."

"Yeah, you've been fine with them. I mean, I guess you've taken that book seriously." Tim gave her a small smile, then hesitated. "I really don't mean people, I guess I mean me."

"You?" Stephanie was dumbfounded. "What did I ever do to you?"

"Nothing! Except give me eight million differ-ent signals. You've acted differently to me every day so far. One day you're super nice, the next day you barely speak to me. Stephanie, I hate games," Tim said.

"But I'm not playing games," Stephanie ob-jected. She felt queasy. This wasn't supposed to be happening!

"Then what do you call it? I thought we had this sort of connection between us. You know, from the first day we met," Tim said. "Now when I try to talk to you, you won't say a word."

"I wanted to talk to you," Stephanie tried to explain. "But I didn't, because I overheard you." She poked at a rock on the ground with her san-dal. "You and Dylan. You told him that you hated it when girls came on strong. And I thought maybe *you* thought I was doing that."

Tim frowned. "Why did you think I was talk-ing about you?"

"Tim, I'd just met you. I thought you were com-plaining about how much time I was spending with you," Stephanie said.

"Actually, that entire conversation had nothing to do with you," Tim said. "Dylan was complain-ing to me about someone else. I was just being sympathetic. Of course, if you'd asked me straight out instead of turning it into some game, you'd have known that."

"I was afraid to ask you," Stephanie admitted. She felt her cheeks turn red with embarrassment. "I'd just met you, and I didn't know you very well, so I just decided to play it cool. To speak only when you spoke to me first. And then not say much," she added.

Now Tim looked embarrassed. "So I guess it was all just a misunderstanding after all," he said.

"I'm sorry I jumped to conclusions," Stephanie said apologetically. She wanted to ask, So do you still like me as much as I like you? Can we go back to where we left off before Cynthia interrupted us? Holding hands, in the moonlight?

But she didn't dare. A few seconds passed.

"So from now on I'll just be me," she ventured. "No more mixed signals."

"That'll be great." Tim's blue eyes gazed intensely at her for a long while. Then he jumped up from the rock he had been sitting on.

"So, do you think we should get back to the rafts?" Tim said. "This is the day we've been waiting for. We don't want to miss any of the fun."

"Definitely not." Stephanie followed Tim down the steep path. She listened absentmindedly as he talked about the Yampa River and the rapids downriver. But she was really thinking about Tim.

So, I guess everything is all right between us, she mused. *He even said he thought we had a connection. And we do. I know we belong together.*

I'll just have to prove it to him!

CHAPTER
12

◆ ◂ ▸ ◆

"Today's the big day," Molly announced when everyone had gathered by the river twenty minutes later. "This is your first Super Summer Adventure Super Challenge. Today, we'll be seeing some *real* rapids. Are you guys ready?"

Cheers and whistles rang out, echoing along the narrow canyon.

"Because this section of the river is very difficult, we're putting you with the people you know best. You need to communicate and stick together," Steve said. "So listen up while we read off the raft assignments!"

When Stephanie heard her name called, she couldn't believe it: she, Kayla, Darcy, Allie, and Anna were all in the same raft!

Normally Stephanie would have been thrilled to have her best friends in a raft with her. But today? They weren't communicating—they weren't even talking. How was that going to help them navigate anything? And Gail was going to be their guide. Gail, who had never given Stephanie a break!

This day is going to be a challenge in more ways than one, Stephanie thought as she walked over to her raft. When she got there, Gail held a paddle out to her.

"You seem to have a knack for rafting, Stephanie. You be the guide today," Gail said.

A knack? Stephanie thought. But what about her crash landing the night before? Had Gail forgotten that already? Or what about the fact that her friends were going to hate having her as a guide? She could picture it now. Her calling out directions, and nobody following them!

"But aren't we going through some Class Four rapids?" Stephanie asked Gail.

"Yes, we're going through Warm Springs and Whirlpool Canyon. And I'll help you, if and when you need it," Gail said. "But I think you're ready to face this challenge on your own."

"Okay . . ." Stephanie said slowly. She didn't know whether to be afraid or grateful that Gail suddenly seemed to have such confidence in her.

Stephanie sat in the back of the raft. One by one, her friends climbed into the boat. Nobody said a word to her.

"Okay, team. Ready?" Gail said as she boarded the raft.

"Ready," they all mumbled.

Some team! Stephanie started steering as they set off down the river. "Um, forward," she commanded in a soft voice.

"Come on, Stephanie. You'll have to be stronger than that," Gail said with a laugh.

Stephanie smiled weakly at her. Gail didn't realize that just sitting in the raft with all of her former friends was taking all the strength she had. "Forward two," she said as they approached some rocks. "Wait! I mean, back one! Back two!"

Stephanie smiled as they missed the rocks. This guiding stuff was fun, once you got started.

"Great!" Gail said. "Keep it up."

Darcy glanced over her shoulder. The expression on her face said it all. She wasn't enjoying taking orders from Stephanie. This wasn't my idea, Stephanie wanted to tell her. But she had to concentrate on the river. She didn't have time to think about her friends, or Tim, or the Flamingoes. They were heading for Whirlpool Canyon!

*   *   *

"Okay, troops. I wanted us all to stop here for a short break," Steve said as Stephanie landed the raft on the bank later that morning. "Have a snack. We have apples and granola bars. Then walk ahead a bit and look at the river. Usually whenever you're about to face a tough rapid, you scout it first. That way you can decide how best to approach it. Knowing what's ahead is half the battle."

Stephanie secured the raft and removed her helmet. Kayla, Darcy, Anna, and Allie quickly grabbed snacks and took off to check out the river. Stephanie found herself walking next to Gail. Her jaw nearly dropped when she saw the rushing white water waiting for them ahead.

"See those little pockets?" Gail pointed to a few areas of swirling water. "Those are holes, where the water's spinning backward. You want to keep away from them. Holes can be almost impossible to escape from.

"Beneath every hole there are lots of sharp rocks. Just remember—miss the holes, and you'll miss the rocks."

"Okay . . ." Stephanie said slowly. But the water seemed to have an endless supply of holes and pockets, judging by the churning water. "Shouldn't *you* start guiding the raft now, Gail?"

"Don't worry, you're doing a great job," Gail reassured her. "You're taking it very seriously, which is important. Your friends have been talking a lot, and you haven't joined in once."

Stephanie smiled faintly. If it were her choice, maybe she'd feel good about it. The fact was, her friends were ignoring her.

"How about this? We'll be co-guides," Gail said. "I'll tell everyone when to paddle—you steer."

"Okay, I guess," Stephanie agreed. She and Gail started back to the raft. When she turned the corner, she saw Darah and Cynthia crouched by her raft, as if they were about to get in.

"What are you doing? That's not your raft," Stephanie said as she went up to them.

"Oh, whoops! You're right, it isn't." Darah shrugged. "Sorry!"

"I told you!" Cynthia swatted Darah on the arm as she slipped something into her pocket.

"Didn't you guys want to scout the rapids?" Gail asked.

"I'd rather be surprised," Darah said. "It'll be more exciting that way."

"Well, good luck, you guys! We'll see you at the bottom," Cynthia said.

Darah giggled. "Exactly."

"What are you talking about?" Stephanie asked.

"We'll see you after the rapids—that's all," Cynthia said.

Stephanie watched them walk away and shook her head. Maybe she and her friends weren't talking. But she'd much rather be in a raft with them than with Darah and Cynthia!

Five minutes later Gail pushed their raft into the river. "Everyone's life jacket on tightly?"

Allie tapped hers. "If this were any tighter, I wouldn't be able to breathe."

"Good. That'll hold you up in case we go over," Gail said. "But don't worry. Whatever happens, we'll be fine."

"Do you really think Stephanie should still be the guide?" Kayla asked. "I saw the rapids and— no offense, Steph. They just look rough, that's all."

"Stephanie and I are sharing guide duties," Gail told her. "We've got it under control."

"Oh. Okay." Kayla turned and gave Stephanie a little smile.

Stephanie returned her smile. Maybe the situation wasn't as hopeless as she thought. Kayla didn't seem to hate her. "I'll be careful," she promised. She stared ahead at the choppy water. She quickly navigated their way around a series of smaller rocks.

"Look out—there's a sharp one!" Gail warned. "Back two!"

Stephanie guided the boat to the left. The raft barely missed the pointed boulder. She started preparing for the big rock at the bend of the river.

"Does anyone else feel like we're sinking?" Darcy asked.

"What?" Stephanie called.

"We're losing air!" Anna said. "The front is lower than the back!"

"You're right—we are sinking!" Gail called. "We must have snagged a rock!"

Stephanie hustled to steer the raft toward shore. She had to get the raft in before they went under!

She couldn't make the boat go in the direction she wanted. Their paddles were useless. She stared at the bottom of the raft. Water was pouring in through a gash!

"Now what?" Stephanie called to Gail.

"Hold on!" Gail shouted to the crew. "Hold on tight! Stay in the boat! Stay in the boat! Stephanie, get the rope bag!"

Stephanie grabbed the rope bag from where it was stowed on the raft floor. She stared at the rushing wall of water coming toward them. The front of the raft went straight up in the air.

Stephanie screamed as Kayla and Anna, sitting in front, were tossed sideways into the river.

Then the raft flipped upside down—and Stephanie tumbled headfirst into the cold, rushing water!

CHAPTER
13

◆ ◀ ▸ ◆

Stephanie felt her body go rigid with shock as she hit the icy water. She struggled against the strong current. *Stay calm*, she told herself. *Swim for the surface*.

She fought to move upward. Her hands touched the rubber raft and she shoved it aside. Giving one last push, she bobbed to the surface.

Stephanie opened her eyes, blurry with water, and tried to get her bearings. She was just to the side of a major rapid!

She tried to swim for shore, but the current pushed her into a rock feetfirst. She grabbed the rock and climbed up on it. She had only been in the water for a minute, but it was so cold she could barely feel her feet.

She spotted Darcy coming up for air. She leaned out and caught her by the arm as her friend almost slid past. "Hold on!"

The water rushed over them as Stephanie tried to pull Darcy out of the water. Darcy struggled to get a grip. Finally, Stephanie managed to get her up and on to the rock, too. There was barely room for both of them.

Darcy crouched beside her. She was panting and coughing. "Where's Kayla?"

"Over there!" Stephanie spotted a yellow life jacket bobbing in the water, downstream. She breathed a sigh of relief. Kayla was swimming for the shore.

"What about Anna?" Darcy searched the water around them frantically. "Where—"

"Gail's got her," Stephanie gasped. She watched as Gail pulled Anna to shore, her arm crooked across Anna's chest. "But where's Allie? I don't see her anywhere!"

"She isn't a good swimmer. I hope she's okay!" Darcy said.

Out of the corner of her eye, Stephanie spotted a flash of orange. She turned in that direction. "Look, it's Allie's life jacket!" she yelled to Darcy. Allie's arms and legs were flailing as the rushing water tossed her around. Allie was stuck in the middle of the rapids!

It's like being in a washing machine, Stephanie remembered Gail saying. *Once you're in a hole, you have no control. Sometimes you can't get out!*

"We have to go in and get her!" Darcy said urgently.

Stephanie glanced downstream. Some of the other campers were trying to paddle back toward them. They would take too long, Stephanie realized. She had a panicky feeling in her chest. She and Darcy had to pull this off on their own!

Stephanie was glad she had managed to grab the rope bag from the raft before it capsized. She pulled rope out of the bottom. "Darcy, tie this to something that won't move."

Darcy looked around frantically. "There isn't anything!" She seemed to be ready to cry.

Stephanie swallowed hard. "Then hold on to it. Tight. And tie the other end to this ring on my life jacket," she instructed.

Darcy's hands shook. She fastened the cord and tied a secure knot. "Stephanie—you can't go in there on your own!"

"What choice do we have? Allie needs us!" Stephanie's voice rose above the pounding waves. "I'll give her the line. You pull her in. Okay? Sit on the rock, so you're more balanced." She took a deep breath, then slid back into the frigid river water.

She saw Allie's head bobbing up now and then. Her lungs were probably full of water. Stephanie fought her way through the waves. She took the cord out of her life jacket. She waited for Allie to surface, then threw the line across the water. "Allie—grab it!" she yelled. "Allie!"

But the rope didn't reach Allie. And Allie was still spinning out of control.

What am I going to do? Stephanie thought helplessly. *Allie's trapped—and I can't do anything about it!*

"Hold on, Stephanie—we're coming!" Molly yelled.

Stephanie saw a raft approaching. Mikki and Jenny were sitting up front. They looked terrified.

"Gail tied our raft to a tree so it won't be swept down the river," Molly yelled above the noisy rapids. "Get on. We'll get Allie!" Stephanie tumbled into the raft, exhausted.

Molly moved the raft closer to the giant rock and hole beneath it. "Mikki, Jenny—paddle as hard as you can!" Molly instructed. "Keep this raft from moving backward!" She joined them in paddling furiously.

Stephanie suddenly saw Allie's arm whirl past in the churning water. She leaned out of the raft and watched Allie's body spin around. Seizing her chance, she grabbed Allie's other arm just as it surfaced.

"I've got your legs, Stephanie!" Molly yelled out. Molly held her in the raft, while Stephanie pulled Allie as hard as she could.

Suddenly Allie popped out of the hole. She was panting and coughing. Her lips were faintly tinged with blue.

"Get her into the boat!" Jenny yelled.

"Hang in there, Allie—come on!" Mikki shouted.

Stephanie dragged Allie over the top of the raft. Molly took a dry blanket out of a waterproof bag and wrapped it around Allie.

Gail and Steve started pulling on the line that held the raft to a tree onshore.

Stephanie just stared at Allie in shock. Was it her fault that Allie almost drowned? Was it the way she had navigated? Was there anything she could have done? But Gail had backed her up all the way, hadn't she?

On their way to shore, they stopped to pick up Darcy from the rock. "Allie, are you okay?" Darcy looked concerned. "Oh, no, your teeth are chattering."

"She's coming around slowly," Molly said. "Probably still numb from shock. Don't worry, you guys are all going to be okay. You'll never forget Whirlpool Canyon. What an experience, right?"

"Sorry," Allie said, speaking for the first time, and coughing. "But I think all I'm going to remember is my lungs being full of water." She coughed again.

"I can't believe how strong the current is," Darcy said. "I've never had to swim in water so rough before."

"Don't worry. Our next adventure is on *dry* land," Molly told her. "Stephanie," she went on, "do you remember going over the rock that tore your raft?"

"We didn't go over any sharp rocks," Stephanie said. "I was careful—I was watching."

"Well, I don't know how else the raft could have been ripped so badly," Molly said. "It has a protective tube so that this can't happen. Let's take a look when we get to shore. Steve managed to haul it in."

Molly maneuvered the raft toward shore, where the other counselors and campers were waiting. When Stephanie climbed out, her legs were shaking. She had used up every last ounce of energy swimming in the cold water.

Kayla and Anna ran up to Allie and hugged her. "You poor thing!" Kayla said.

Stephanie watched her friends hug. She wanted

to join in, but obviously wasn't invited. She headed over to check the damaged raft.

Tim rushed up to her. "Stephanie! Are you okay?" he asked with concern.

"Oh, yeah. I'm fine," Stephanie said. She felt numb, and her teeth were chattering.

Tim put a hand on her arm. "Wow, your skin is freezing cold. Here, wear this." He took off his red fleece jacket and draped it over her shoulders.

"Thanks," Stephanie said. She pulled the jacket around her.

"I'm glad you guys made it out," he said. "That was really scary to watch."

Stephanie was about to tell him how scary it felt, when Molly called to her. "Stephanie, come check out your raft!"

She zipped up the warm fleece jacket over her wet clothes and hurried over to the raft. A group of campers were gathered around it.

The raft was lying upside down. A series of gashes went all the way from the bow to the stern.

"That's odd. I've never seen that many tears before," Steve commented.

"They must have been made by a very sharp rock," Gail suggested.

Tim stared at the rips. "Or a knife," he said.

"What are you talking about?" Steve asked.

"Look at how smooth the edges are," Tim said.

"If a rock cut the raft, wouldn't the edges of the holes be sort of jagged and uneven?"

"Maybe," Gail agreed. "But what are you suggesting? That a knife was floating in the river? That's highly unlikely."

"I know that didn't happen," Stephanie said. "Because I know exactly where the knife was." She turned and pointed at Darah. "In her pocket. She has a pink Swiss Army knife. I've seen it, and I'm sure she used it."

"What? Everyone on this trip has a Swiss Army knife. It was on our suggested packing list!" Darah said. "Don't be ridiculous."

"You guys threatened to get revenge on me," Stephanie said. "And today you decided to carry it out by deliberately cutting holes in our raft. You were hanging around it when we took a break to scout the rapids. I saw you put something in your pocket when I walked up. And you were laughing about seeing us at the bottom!"

"What? Are you crazy?" Darah said. "We meant we'd see you at the end of the trip."

"You ran into a rock," Cynthia said with a shrug. "It's not your fault you don't know how to guide a raft yet. I mean, no one would blame you for not knowing what to do."

"I didn't run into anything! This raft has layers. It's incredibly hard to tear. This wouldn't just happen. It was no accident!" Stephanie insisted. "And you did it because you thought I was playing all those practical jokes on you. That's what everyone thinks." She looked at Gail. "But everyone's wrong. I'm innocent!"

For a minute no one said anything. All Stephanie could hear was the rushing river behind her.

Finally Gail spoke up. "There's no evidence to suggest that what happened to your raft has anything to do with the pranks, Stephanie. I think you're jumping to conclusions."

"*I* think Stephanie's right," Allie said defiantly. "I don't think this was an accident, either."

"And I know she wasn't behind any of the pranks," Kayla said. "We share a tent. I'd know if she was up to something."

Stephanie felt the corners of her mouth turn up in a smile. It was an odd feeling. She hadn't smiled all day. Her friends were actually coming to *her* rescue. Even after the way she'd accused them at the campfire the night before!

"Well, okay, so maybe it wasn't just Stephanie. Maybe it was all you guys together," Darah said. "And you keep blaming each other as a way of, like, distracting attention from any one person, but—"

"No, Darah," Darcy interrupted. "That sounds more like something you guys would do. We're innocent. But I've been thinking about the pranks. I think you guys pulled them yourselves, and the reason you did it was to frame *us*. That way we'd get in trouble and you'd get a bunch of attention."

Stephanie was stunned. She'd never considered that possibility before. But it was almost crazy enough to make sense.

"I don't know what you're talking about," Cynthia said.

"That's a pretty wild theory," Mikki agreed. "Maybe you've been spending too much time thinking, Darcy."

"Far too much time thinking," Steve broke in. "As Gail just said, there's no evidence to prove—"

"It isn't just Darcy," Anna said, ignoring Steve. "We all discussed it. There was one thing that didn't add up. Cynthia got frogs in her sleeping bag; Tiffany turned green in the shower; Mikki got scared by a bear; Jenny got swamped in the raft. But nothing ever happened to you, Darah."

"Yeah, because I was *lucky!*" Darah cried. "Because you guys ran out of ideas."

"No, that's not it," Kayla said. "It's because you planned it all. Why would you want to make yourself suffer?"

"Wow," Stephanie breathed. "You guys are totally on to something. I can't believe I didn't think of it before. It's so obvious."

"The only thing that's obvious is that you've all lost your minds!" Darah cried. She looked around at the circle of campers and counselors. "None of you is actually *listening* to this crazy theory, are you?"

"Yes, we *are* listening, and we'll think about what everyone has said," Steve replied. "But I'm afraid we don't have time to work this all out right now. We need to get back on the river so we can meet up with the vans and wrap up this trip tonight."

"We're scheduled to stay at a youth hostel," Gail said. "Which means a hot meal, beds, showers—"

"What are we waiting for? Let's go!" Darah and Tiffany started dragging their raft into the water.

Molly laughed. "I don't remember seeing them that motivated about *anything* before." She turned to Stephanie. "You and your friends will split up and each go into a different raft."

Stephanie nodded. "Okay, we'll sort ourselves out once everyone else gets in." She started down to the water, her friends close behind.

Stephanie paused before wading into the river toward the rafts. "Thanks for backing me up," she told everyone. "And I'm sorry about accusing you last night, and for not believing you earlier."

"That's okay." Darcy put her helmet back on.

"I shouldn't have made fun of you for pledging to leave the Flamingoes alone. You said it, and you meant it. You won our bet, Stephanie. I owe you three weeks of hard labor."

Stephanie laughed. "Having someone else do my chores sounds awfully good right now," she said. "But I'm not sure I deserve it. I did mean my pledge, five days ago," Stephanie said. "But now I don't know."

"What?" Kayla stopped in the middle of fastening her life jacket's straps. "Are you giving up on ignoring them?"

"I can't ignore them! Not if they're going to put us in danger like they just did." Stephanie looked over her shoulder at Gail and Molly. "I don't care what anyone says. That raft was deliberately sabotaged. I can't look the other way after something like that."

"How about if we make another pledge?" Darcy asked. "We won't *start* anything. But if they try something else, then I hereby give us permission to get revenge."

Each girl placed her hand over the others. "Deal," Stephanie said.

CHAPTER
14

◆ ◀ ◢ ◆

Steve stood up at the counselors' table. He rapped his fork against a glass to get everyone's attention.

"So, how good did that hot shower feel?" he asked once the room was quiet.

"I thought I'd never get clean again," Allie said.

Stephanie laughed. "You're loving all this roughing it, aren't you?"

"Not exactly," Allie said with a frown.

"Come on, you're having fun—admit it," Kayla teased her.

"Oh, sure. Sleeping on the ground. Nearly drowning. It's been a real blast." Allie smiled. "What's next?"

"Well, campers, our hearty congratulations on

surviving your first challenge," Steve continued. "There are plenty more where that came from!"

Stephanie stole a glance at the table where the Flamingoes were sitting. There were official trip challenges, and then there were other challenges. Like dealing with Flamingoes!

Steve cleared his throat. "Now that everyone's had a chance to clean up and chow down, we have a few announcements to make. First, we want to let you know that our next adventure will be a backpacking trip in the Colorado Rockies," Steve said.

"Great!" Darcy looked at Stephanie. Her eyes were shining with excitement.

"Cool." Stephanie couldn't wait for the hiking trip.

"Unfortunately," Steve continued, "due to some of the problems we encountered during our rafting trip, five campers won't be coming with us."

Darcy gasped.

Stephanie felt her heart start beating faster. She stared at her friends around the table. One, two, three, four . . . and she was number five. They were sending five campers home?

"I should never have taken the Flamingoes' bags," Stephanie muttered. "If we get kicked out, this is all my fault."

"No, it isn't," Allie said. "We're all in this together."

"Now, I hear lots of whispering out there, so let me put your minds at ease," Gail said. She stood next to Steve. "If you're in this room, you're *staying* on the trip."

"Yes!" Stephanie screamed. She and Kayla exchanged high-fives, as everyone else in the room cheered.

Then, all of a sudden, Stephanie stopped celebrating. "Wait a second. The Flamingoes are in this room," she said. "So they're not leaving, either."

"Then who got kicked off the trip?" Darcy stood up to survey the dining room.

"As you're all aware, someone was playing a series of practical jokes on a group of girls," Gail said. "A lot of accusations were made. Nobody knew who was behind the pranks. Well, we started playing detective yesterday, and finally, the pranksters tipped their hands. We caught them this afternoon when they tried to pull off practical joke number five—on Darah. We're talking about Bruce, Kevin, Tyler, Aaron, and Sammy."

Stephanie's eyes widened. "Bruce! It was him and his friends all along?"

"They packed some interesting supplies for this

trip," Steve explained. "They brought along the bear slipper that scared Mikki, the green goop for Tiffany's shower, the baby oil that made Stephanie slip in the raft, and they caught the frogs for Cynthia's sleeping bag at the lake near our first campsite. They admitted they were planning on tricking *somebody* before they even started the trip. They just didn't know who. Apparently they picked you girls." He looked at the Flamingoes and shrugged. "I have no idea why."

"I do," Allie whispered to Stephanie. "Remember how rude Cynthia was to them the first day— especially Bruce?"

"The boys have already been taken to the bus station," Gail said. "We were sorry to have to ask them to leave. We don't enjoy sending campers home, and we don't want to have to do it again this summer."

Molly stood up. She held a long spoon in her hand. "And now for the fun part of this meeting. Dessert! We have all the fixings for make-your-own sundaes, so come on up!"

Chairs scraped against the floor as campers scrambled toward the ice cream. Three giant tubs had just been brought out from the kitchen, with bottles of toppings and cans of whipped cream.

"Let's wait a few minutes," Allie said. "Some

126

of those boys would knock us down to get to the hot fudge."

Stephanie only half heard her. She was too busy figuring out what happened over the past few days. "I can't believe it," she mused. "Bruce deliberately framed us, to shift suspicion away from himself. He even got me to accuse you, so we wouldn't trust each other."

"He definitely framed us," Anna said slowly. "But how would he get that idea?"

"I think I know how. He was sitting in front of me, that first day in the van, when I was telling Tim about all our problems with the Flamingoes," Stephanie said. "I was so upset that the Flamingoes were on the trip that I told Tim the whole story. He was giving me advice on how to deal with them. The whole time, Bruce must have been plotting how to deal with them himself—especially after they were so mean to him!"

"He knew he could frame us, because we had such a history with the Flamingoes," Kayla concluded. "And in the process he was playing a big practical joke on us, too. The creep."

"Imagine if they hadn't caught him. We'd be on the bus home right now, instead of them," Anna said angrily.

"I guess the trip organizers will pull some people off the waiting list," Darcy said. "Maybe we'll get a group of boys who are actually cute *and* nice."

"Come on, there are cute boys here," Stephanie said.

"Sure, there's Tim. But he's already taken," Darcy said meaningfully.

"Actually, Tim and I had a misunderstanding," Stephanie admitted. "But I think we've cleared it up." She told her friends about her talk with Tim earlier that day.

"I think we understand each other much better now," she finished up. "And he was totally nice after our rafting accident today." She hugged Tim's red fleece jacket that she was wearing.

"Gee, Steph, that's great." Allie beamed at Stephanie.

Gail walked up to her. She held a sundae in her hand. "Do you like hot fudge?" she asked.

"I love it," Stephanie said.

"Great! Because this is for you." She handed the sundae dish to Stephanie.

"For me?" Stephanie stared at the gooey hot fudge and melting whipped cream. "Thanks. But, um, why?"

"Because I'm sorry I didn't trust you," Gail said. "You obviously had nothing to do with the pranks—once the trip started. But there *was* that incident with the luggage."

"I know." Stephanie nodded. "I won't make that mistake again."

"That's great. I'll get your camera back to you first thing tomorrow. Sorry I kept it so long. And good job paddling," Gail said. She patted Stephanie's shoulder and moved on to talk to other campers.

"Wow. I never knew Gail could be so nice," Allie commented.

"I know!" Stephanie took a big bite of the sundae.

Darcy didn't look so enthused. "It's nice to have Gail off your back, but why won't anyone believe us when we say it wasn't a rock?"

"Let me guess. Because you're completely unbelievable?" Stephanie turned and saw Darah standing behind them.

"Unbelievable? Speak for yourself, Darah," Darcy shook her head. "We'll never believe you again after that little trick you pulled on us this afternoon. You know, the one with the raft?"

The five Flamingoes looked at one another. Darah shrugged her shoulders. "Actually, if you want the whole story—"

Mikki broke up laughing. "The *whole* story? Get it?"

"No, I don't." Stephanie frowned at her. "What are you talking about?"

"H-o-l-e? We did rip your raft," Darah admitted.

"Only you weren't supposed to sink." Cynthia wrinkled her nose. "Just sort of deflate."

"I guess we put in too many holes," Jenny suggested.

"But, hey, all's well that ends well," Tiffany said brightly.

"Of all the dirty tricks . . . I almost drowned!" Allie fumed. "I'm telling Gail right now!"

"Hold on, Allie—wait!" Stephanie grabbed her sleeve. "Don't say anything to Gail."

"What? Why shouldn't she?" Darcy asked. "We can get them kicked off the trip!"

"But we don't have any proof. If you bring Gail over here, they'll deny everything, and nothing will change," Stephanie went on. She'd just managed to earn Gail's trust. She didn't want to lose it. "We have to let this go. Forget about it."

"I told you guys Stephanie was the smart one," Darah said. "She obviously knows when to quit."

Stephanie smiled at her. "I'm not giving up. I'm just waiting for a better opportunity, that's all."

"Let it go," Darcy repeated. "You're serious, aren't you?"

Stephanie nodded. She remembered what Tim had said. This wasn't worth fighting over.

"I don't know why I'm doing this. I guess I

must trust you," Darcy said. "Okay. We'll forget about it," she told the Flamingoes.

"Whatever," Tiffany said.

"Like we were worried." Cynthia flipped her hair over her shoulder.

"Come on, guys. The ice cream's melting," Jenny said. She led the group away.

"So now what?" Allie asked after they were gone. "I mean, we can't just *ignore* them. That's too dangerous."

"All we can do is watch them. And next time, we won't let them get the better of us," Stephanie said. "That's another promise I'll keep." She tossed her empty ice cream dish into a trash can. "I'll see you guys later. There's something else I need to do."

Tim was standing by the door, talking to some other campers. She headed over, wending her way around chairs and tables. When she got close enough to him, she tapped him on the shoulder. "Hi."

"Hey, Steph. What's up?" he asked, turning around.

"I just wanted to thank you for giving me this earlier, on the river." Stephanie held out the fleece jacket. "It really helped. I was freezing!"

"Oh, you're welcome. No problem." Tim took the jacket and tied it around his waist. "So. That was pretty weird, about Bruce and his friends, wasn't it?'' he asked.

''Definitely,'' Stephanie said.

''I'm sorry some people blamed you,'' Tim said. ''They should have seen you had nothing to do with it.''

''How could they know?'' Stephanie shrugged her shoulders. ''We all just met.''

''But *I* just met you,'' Tim said. ''And I never thought you did it. I knew you were trying to get along with the Flamingoes.''

Stephanie flushed with pleasure. It was nice to know Tim thought she was making an effort.

''Anyhow, I've gotten to know some of them, and the Flamingoes aren't so bad after all.'' Tim laughed. ''Some of them can even be nice.''

I hope he's not referring to Cynthia, Stephanie thought. To change the subject, she said, ''So, how about that backpacking trip? Are you up for it?''

''I'm totally psyched,'' Tim said.

Stephanie took a deep breath. *Be yourself*, she thought. *Tell Tim what you're really thinking.* Aloud, she said, ''Wouldn't it be great if we could hike together? In the same group, I mean?''

''Yeah, that would be cool.'' Tim shifted from one foot to the other. ''We can see about that tomorrow. After we get a good night's sleep. I'm beat.''

"So am I," Stephanie said, beaming. "Good night."

She rushed out of the dining room and ran upstairs to her dorm room. Then, lying on her cot, she took out her journal.

Everything's working out just the way I want it to! My friends and I are together again. And now I know Tim really likes me! From now on, I'll always be myself. No more games. I know that Tim and I belong together—we're a perfect couple.

I can't believe how wonderful everything is! And we have more than three weeks of Super Summer Adventure to come!

"Hey, Stephanie, come outside with us!" Kayla appeared in the doorway. "There's an amazing moon out there!"

Stephanie put her journal on the bed and followed Kayla out the front door of the hostel. She stared up into the night sky.

The largest full moon she had ever seen glowed brilliantly above her. In the distance, mountains rose majestically against the horizon. Stephanie drew her breath in sharply. The view was totally awesome.

"Hey, guys." Darcy put a hand on Stephanie's

shoulder. "This is why we came on this trip. To see amazing sights like this one."

"To go on the coolest adventures ever!" Anna added.

"And to be together!" Stephanie finished up.

"And we'll never allow anything to come between us again!" Allie exclaimed. "Group hug, everyone!"

The five friends put their arms around one another for a long while.

"I don't know about you guys, but I'm pooped," Kayla said when they broke up. "See you all in the morning."

Stephanie drifted away from the others. She felt too excited to go to bed. She thought about everything that had happened that day. Capsizing in Whirlpool Canyon. Making up with her friends. Getting together with Tim. And tomorrow she and Tim would start a whole new adventure together.

Stephanie wandered down the path that led away from the hostel. She could hear other kids talking and laughing in the distance. She rounded a bend in the path.

Then she stopped dead in her tracks.

Two people stood in the moonlight, so close together that their heads were almost touching.

One was Tim.

The other, holding his hand and gazing up into his eyes, was Cynthia!

Stephanie stared in shock. Her stomach gave a sickening lurch.

Oh, no, Stephanie thought. *I can't lose Tim to a Flamingo!*

FULL HOUSE™
Michelle

#5: THE GHOST IN MY CLOSET 53573-0/$3.99
#6: BALLET SURPRISE 53574-9/$3.99
#7: MAJOR LEAGUE TROUBLE 53575-7/$3.99
#8: MY FOURTH-GRADE MESS 53576-5/$3.99
#9: BUNK 3, TEDDY, AND ME 56834-5/$3.99
#10: MY BEST FRIEND IS A MOVIE STAR!
        (Super Edition) 56835-3/$3.99
#11: THE BIG TURKEY ESCAPE 56836-1/$3.99
#12: THE SUBSTITUTE TEACHER 00364-X/$3.99
#13: CALLING ALL PLANETS 00365-8/$3.99
#14: I'VE GOT A SECRET 00366-6/$3.99
#15: HOW TO BE COOL 00833-1/$3.99
#16: THE NOT-SO-GREAT OUTDOORS 00835-8/$3.99
#17: MY HO-HO-HORRIBLE CHRISTMAS 00836-6/$3.99
MY AWESOME HOLIDAY FRIENDSHIP BOOK
(An Activity Book) 00840-4/$3.99
FULL HOUSE MICHELLE OMNIBUS 02181-8/$6.99
#18: MY ALMOST PERFECT PLAN 00837-4/$3.99
#19: APRIL FOOLS 01729-2/$3.99
#20: MY LIFE IS A THREE-RING CIRCUS 01730-6/$3.99
#21: WELCOME TO MY ZOO 01731-4/$3.99
#22: THE PROBLEM WITH PEN PALS 01732-2/$3.99
#23: MERRY CHRISTMAS, WORLD! 02098-6/$3.99
#24: TAP DANCE TROUBLE 02154-0/$3.99
MY SUPER SLEEPOVER BOOK 02701-8/$3.99

A MINSTREL BOOK   Published by Pocket Books

Simon & Schuster Mail Order Dept. BWB
200 Old Tappan Rd., Old Tappan, N.J. 07675

Please send me the books I have checked above. I am enclosing $_____ (please add $0.75 to cover the
postage and handling for each order. Please add appropriate sales tax). Send check or money order–no cash or C.O.D.'s please. Allow up to
six weeks for delivery. For purchase over $10.00 you may use VISA: card number, expiration date and customer signature must be included.

Name _____

Address _____

City _____ State/Zip _____

VISA Card # _____ Exp.Date _____

Signature _____

1033-29

FULL HOUSE™

SISTERS

A brand-new series starring Stephanie AND Michelle!

#1 Two On The Town

Stephanie and Michelle find themselves
in the big city—and in big trouble!

#2 One Boss Too Many

Stephanie and Michelle think camp will be major fun.
If only these two sisters were getting along!

When sisters get together...expect the unexpected!

 A MINSTREL® BOOK
Published by Pocket Books

2012-01